DADDY, PLEASE DON'T KILL MY MAMA

Novel

Natisha P. Parsons

Mwanaka Media and Publishing Pvt Ltd,
Chitungwiza, Zimbabwe
*
Creativity, Wisdom, and Beauty

Publisher: *Mmap*
Mwanaka Media and Publishing Pvt Ltd
24 Svosve Road, Zengeza 1
Chitungwiza, Zimbabwe
mwanaka@yahoo.com
mwanaka13@gmail.com
https://www.mmapublishing.org
www.africanbookscollective.com/publishers/mwanaka-media-and-publishing
https://facebook.com/MwanakaMediaAndPublishing/

Distributed in and outside N. America by African Books Collective
orders@africanbookscollective.com
www.africanbookscollective.com

ISBN: 978-1-77933-146-5
EAN: 9781779331465

DISCLAIMER
All views expressed in this publication are those of the author and do not
necessarily reflect the views of *Mmap*.

Part 1
In the Beginning

Jordan worked for a car repair company that opened up not far from their suburban farm home. Time passed fairly uneventfully, and before they knew it, there were six children and no two of them fully two years apart!

Jordan soon worked his way up to foreman. He was honest and reliable. Soon he was running the place because Stefan, the boss, a grossly obese man, preferred to stay at home with meat and liquor at his elbow, watching sport on the TV. His long-suffering wife, Elena, did the books and answered the telephone. The small staff looked to Jordan for direction and instruction. Even Elena treated Jordan like he was the boss.

Home was like running a crèche and Sylvia decided to put her never-used Day Care skills to the test. After a discussion, placing the logistics on the table, discussing the pros and cons of turning home into a workplace, they decided it would work. It was more successful than they both expected. Jordan marketed for her at work and before they knew it word-of-mouth brought in ten children not counting their own.

Sylvia needed help. She also needed more space. Jordan solved that by getting a park home that he converted into a suitable place with the help of his workmates over a weekend. Soon Sylvia was the proud owner of a nifty crèche in her very own yard. And help seemed to fall right into their hands. Jordan came home from work, with a timely proposition for his wife.

"Honey, there's a new guy at work who needs place to stay like yesterday. Why don't we let him fix the outbuilding and he can use it."

"That dilapidated old house? It's probably infested with creepy crawlies of every description. It'll cost, honey. We can't spare the cash, can we?"

"He's prepared to fix it. I told him …he's willing to fix it. They needn't pay rent, just utilities."

"Who's he and does he have a family?"

"He's Taylor de Vee and his wife is Elizabeth. They have two-three children… not sure; around James and Livvie's ages… I could be wrong."

James and Olivia were around eight and ten at the time. Olivia was almost eleven months older than James and Kay just on a year younger than him. Luke and Andrew came next. Their baby, Sonya was three and a bit when the crèche got going. Turned out the de Vee children were five, four and three. Sidney and Cohen were born in the same year. They were quite immature for their ages and, when she got to know them better, Sylvia put it down to the fear that pervaded their very psyches, due to an out-of-control father. She was convinced their father's excessive drinking was the root of the problem.

Sylvia thought about it for a second. "If you work with him and can vouch for his character, then I don't see why not… and on the other hand, Jor, what about the repairing of that old place? Even for the two of you it's too much…"

"No problem. We'll get the men at work to pitch in, like they did with the crèche. They must have stuff in their sheds and back yards.

4

And they have muscles." He held up his arms and clenched his fists. "Man power, Sylvie, me gal, man power. Lotsa that between us. I'll talk to them." He took the phone off the wall and called Taylor. "He'll be here later today…"

"Jordan, it's late already. Why not put it off till tomorrow?"

"He's too excited, Syl. I don't want to throw cold water on his eagerness."

"I s'pose."

Taylor arrived in a rattletrap of an old van, his wife and three children all squashed together alongside him. He, a short man, wiry, almost completely bald and as toothless as a new born baby! His bald pate glowed a much darker hue thanks to the setting sun's rays. His rugged features made it hard to guess even his approximate age. Yet there was a charm about him that Sylvia realised is what maybe drew Elizabeth. When he smiled and his large almost black eyes just about disappeared, he exuded a definite magnetic charm. She, at least six inches taller than he, slightly lighter skinned, red-haired and beautiful with just a hint of make-up, could have been a model if she chose. Their three beautiful children were an interesting cross between them. All three had large gleaming dark eyes, thickly framed by long, dark curling lashes. There was an air of nervousness about them and they clung to their mother. The youngest, a little girl, had a thumb in her mouth.

Their raucous father introduced them, roughly pulling them from where they cringed behind their mom. Taylor spoke with a strong Afrikaans accent. "This is Sidney, my first born… daddy's boy…" Sidney screwed up his face and scowled at him. Then he looked shyly at Sylvia and held out his hand.

"And this is Cohen. He's ou lang-one. Taller than his older brother…look at him. He'll play basketball one day and make us all rich… and heppe-e-e-…yippee-ee-ee! And…come here, you," he snatched up his daughter and threw her up into the air. She shrieked with fear, her face registering stark terror. "Don't…" Sylvia shouted, involuntarily, stretching out her arms. "Are you stark, staring mad? The child is terrified."

Elizabeth reached out nervously, hoarsely uttering, "Cora! My child!"

The man laughed again. "A-a-a-g, Mrs Sylvie, she's ok. She's used of it. Nē, Cora, papa's baby?" He bent to comfort the crying child. "An' this is Deddie's baby: Cora. Cora, say hello to Mrs Sylvie."

Sylvia was surprised to smell alcohol on the man's breath. "I bet a whole year's wages his wife looks so sour because she's embarrassed… she has to visit people – potential landlords to boot – with a man who's been drinking," Sylvia told herself. "I wonder if his good cheer is from the bottle. Or maybe he doesn't need Dutch courage to be cheerful?" The smell of liquor on someone always made her jittery. It got her insides in a knot and her breathing awkward. Worse, it roused childhood memories best left undisturbed.

The children soon got together and the Madden little ones had the de Vee children on their sturdy, brightly painted Dad-made seesaw, slide and jungle gym. Their joyful screams filled the air.

Elizabeth expressed alarm at first for her children were not accustomed to outdoor structural toys.

"Ag, leave them, sweet pie, they won't fall further than the ground." His huge, toothless guffaw would have had Sylvia laughing along if she did not sense an unpleasant undercurrent. *Just what is it I am sensing?* she asked herself. Little Sonja was strapped to her back and she felt the need to put her down. "Go join the others," she playfully patted her bottom and off the little one scampered, shouting excitedly.

Sylvia was polite to the man. Animatedly they planned what changes they would make in addition to the repairs. In her mind she was busy plotting ways of escape from the men.

Periodically Taylor turned to Elizabeth and said, "Né, sweet pie?" to which she replied, "Of course, dear." Her smile never reached her large hazel eyes.

Soon Sylvia made her excuses. "Jordan, I'm off to make us something to drink."

"Off you go, then," Taylor called out. "An' make mine a beer...ice cold and frothy." *Cheeky!*

His huge spluttery laugh had Jordan in stitches. Sylvia smiled coldly. Jordan winked at her. Elizabeth scowled at her husband. "Hey, this is not the pub, you!" Jordan playfully slapped Taylor on the back. "We be teetotallers, my man... you know... sober sides. It's a hot drink, so name yours."

"Coffee, sweet and black and strong, like my beautiful wife." More laughter. Elizabeth turned red. Sylvia put an arm around her and they walked away. "It's off to the kitchen for us girls...you know...where we belong."

"There's a girl that know her place." The man laughed loudly and long.

A disgusted Sylvia ignored him. "Come, Elizabeth, let's see if the biscuit jars got something in it. I'm sure these busy-busy men could use some biscuits and coffee."

As soon as they were out of earshot, Sylvia said, "Elizabeth, woman to woman, what am I sensing here?"

"I'm not gonna play with words, Sylvia; it's exactly as you suspect. Taylor's a man's man and at home he's a nasty bully. My body has blotches old, new and very old. My ribs feel like they wanna fall apart. My black eye is healing and this bit of colour does a good job hiding it. He threatened to kill me if I as much as tried to walk out. I know he means it because I know him. We'll be kicked out from here, too, before long and he knows it." Her eyes filled with tears and the compassionate Sylvia determined there and then they would get the outhouse so they could be close and she could be a friend to this poor, poor mistreated woman.

The renovations began the following day. Sylvia had spoken to Jordan about Taylors drinking habits but Jordan said they wouldn't be in each other's hair so it wouldn't matter. Sidney, Cohen and Cora were charming children and they would all get on well together.

Before the week ended the de Vees arrived with their things piled onto the back of their van and the boys seated precariously amongst them. Cora was on her mother's lap.

Elizabeth looked pitifully at Sylvia when they arrived. She had a layer of make-up under the right eye and along the jaw that failed to achieve its purpose. Sylvia's heart sank.

Sylvia's Day Care Centre was satisfying yet exhausting! Elizabeth's arrival was heaven-sent. Sylvia appreciated having another woman to talk to. Woman things just cannot be satisfactorily discussed with a husband and children no matter how much you loved them. And here was another woman on her very doorstep. Could life be any better?

Life went on as well as one can expect, living out on a farm, raising six children and running a crèche. The lives of the de Vee and Madden children became happily meshed together. The de Vee children were more at home at the Madden home than in their own unhappy one.

Frequently, at dead of night, the de Vee's sought shelter from the rampaging, drunken Taylor at the Madden's. At first, he didn't go near to look for his family, but, familiarity being the catalyst that breeds contempt, he soon violated their privacy. Sylvia was aghast. She sent him away with a flea in his ear. He docilely complied.

The first time.

Thereafter he stood under the huge oak tree not far from the kitchen door, and called out obscenities at the top of his voice. "What a desecration," Sylvia said to Jordan. "Good thing we don't have neighbours. Phew! They'd be calling the police, that's for sure."

"Much good that'd do. He's got friends in all the places. Don't take any notice of him, love. It's the booze talking. He'll quieten down just now. Be a good thing if he left off drinking. I'll have a serious talk with him tomorrow."

"Maybe he needs professional help. This is a bit much of a muchness."

Jordan did talk to him but all it achieved was a slight change in his tactics. He remembered to keep away from the Madden residence when his family had escaped his fire and vice.

This added a new dimension to the lives of the Madden children. Seeing a father behave in this way made them realise what a good man their father was. Kay, with her growing wit and wisdom, obtained James's assistance and together they made a wooden plaque, inscribed in words painstakingly burnt in with a long nail with a thickly padded handle: IN THIS HOUSE LIVES A GOOD MA[dde]N, and put it up on their front verandah gate. Jordan laughed indulgently but felt proud that his children regarded him in that light. Sylvia approved their children's sentiments… completely.

Sidney de Vee made a cardboard plaque that read IN THIS HOUSE LIVES A BAD, BAD MAN. His mother destroyed it angrily. "Respect your father!"

"He doesn't deserve it, Ma," Sidney said sulkily and his brother nodded vigorously.

"Deserve it? Deserve it? You respect unconditionally because of who *you* are, not because of what others do or don't do! If you cannot respect him for himself, do so because the Bible instructs you to do so."

"Ma, the Bible also says that our parents mustn't push us to do wrong, an' Dad's pushing us… seriously."

"Why don't we go to church, Ma? Why?" Sidney wanted to know. "Have we ever been to church? I can' remember."

Cohen and Cora joined in. "I also want to go to church," Cora whined. "Ma, I wanna go to church. There's a girl in my class an' she always tells us about God and Jesus."

"What's her name?" Cohen wanted to know.

"Camilla…"

"I know… she's Manuel's sister. He acts so holy-holy, we always laugh at him." Cohen began to guffaw.

"Watch yourself, my boy. Its boys like Manuel that grow up to be the opposite of your father! What do you want to grow up to be?"

"Ja, jus' ask him, Ma." Cora jeered at her embarrassed brother. He twisted in his seat and apologized to his mother.

"Don't apologise to me, Son. Treat Manuel with respect. Try to copy his values. Lord knows you're exposed to the worst side of a man right in your own home."

One Sunday afternoon Jordan, Taylor and Elizabeth took the children to the zoo. Sonja was not too well so Sylvia decided to stay home with her. The over-the-counter medicine from the chemist had made her drowsy and Sylvia was feeling lonely.

She went into Sonja's room and was soon fast asleep beside her. She dreamt of luxurious living in suburbia, with every mod con one could possibly think of. She was relaxed on a chaise longue, and a neatly clad maid was waiting on her. The drinks tray she carried was laden with ice encrusted glasses, ice cubes tinkling pleasingly as she walked. The pool just beyond them shimmered invitingly in the mid-morning sun.

Jordan was on a chaise alongside her. She looked at him but this was not her Jordan! This lecherous stranger who smiled sickeningly at her was definitely not her husband. His eyes were unmistakably Taylor's! He raised his glass to her and she just knew it held an alcoholic drink. The shock woke her up. Her heart was beating fast and her breathing was disturbed. "Calm down," she sternly told herself. "It was just a dream... a nasty one, but just a dream!"

Carefully she slid off the bed and went to the kitchen to make a batch of scones for the revellers and to down a much-needed cup of tea. The dream just would not leave her alone. What could it mean?

"It means, Sylvia Madden, you need castor oil!" she crossly said out loud.

Sipping the scalding tea while she waited for the scones to bake, she imagined what the zoo visitors were up to. She let her imagination run wild until she imagined Taylor falling into the lions' pit. She shook her head violently and got to her feet. "That's evil!" she scolded herself.

When the family got home, noisy, excited, with lots of feed-back for Mama, she enjoyed anew the excitement of her children.

The children grew up healthy, well adjusted, loving and respectful towards their parents and each other. The Madden's were known to be a kind, loving family. The parents of the children at 'Aunt Sylvia's' were pleased that their children were being raised by such a good woman.

One morning Taylor popped in to tell Sylvia that Elizabeth would not be in to work as she had developed a bad cough and a streaming nose. "You should see what my poor wife look like, Sylvie. This flu is really bed... really bed... I mus'n cetch it or the chu'ren." He would bring medicine from the doctor after work, he promised looking as sad as three days of rainy weather. Emphatically he advised Ollie not to go near. "She's cetchy, you know, en you en the chu'ren mus'n get it."

"Thanks for letting me know," she said coldly, and closed the door.

Overnight!? Sylvia did not believe a word. "What's the ogre been up to now?" she asked herself.

"We shall see what we shall see," she told herself as she hung her apron on the hook behind the kitchen door.

Leaving her head nanny in charge, she went to visit Elizabeth as soon as it was convenient.

"Elizabeth," she shouted, knocking at her bedroom window, "I don't believe a word of what Taylor told me! Open the door."

"Please, Sylvie, go away," a muffled voice called out. "I'm too sick. You'll take germs away to the children."

"Tommy rot! Open this door or I *will* break it down, I swear."

"Please don't do that," a frantic Elizabeth jumped up from bed, making the springs creak noisily.

Elizabeth presented a sorry sight. Sylvia burst into a shocked, angry, prolonged wail. She battled to get her breath back letting out whimpering sounds like a whipped child. Her hands worked as though they had a life of their own. She was stupefied. Elizabeth's eyes were completely swollen, blue, purple and red. Her mouth was hugely swollen. She was grotesque! She walked like a badly arthritic eighty-year old.

When she could function, Sylvia burst out with every ugly word she knew. Elizabeth just stood there like a statue, staring at the distraught woman, listening to the tidal wave of anger. She never knew Sylvia had it in her; nor did Sylvia.

"Let's get you looking better. It's off to the clinic with you. Now! But first let's go make up your bed, and air the place. It stinks… of Taylor!" Elizabeth tried to protest but she was too weak to stop Sylvia. The frail hand she stretched out Sylvia ignored.

Sylvia grabbed hold of the bedding and yanked it all off in one swift movement. Something flew up from the bed hit the wall, and bounced back down onto the mattress. Sylvia stared at it. Then the familiarity of the shape dawned on her. She remembered the way Elizabeth was walking.

"Oh my dear, dear, God!" she exploded in utter disbelief. "Is this what I think it is?"

Elizabeth looked down and began to sob anew…great, big, shuddering sobs that pulled at Sylvia's heartstrings. She sank down beside the utterly humiliated woman crumbled in a pathetic heap on the floor. All she could do was rock her like a baby and allow her to sob her humiliation out. "S-s-s-so de-gra-gra-grading," she managed to stammer.

"Hush, dear one, don't say anything. This is the work of evil…evil. You won't be its victim forever." She sang little nursery songs to soothe the aching, hurting battered woman. Will she ever recover from this? He deserves the death penalty… by slow torture. Sylvia struggled to overcome the hate and anger that filled her as she sang softly and rocked gently. Pictures floated in her head of just how he should be put to death.

Eventually Elizabeth's agony eased and Sylvia helped her onto the couch. Slowly she explained that his drinking had taken its toll and Taylor was unable to perform as he thought he could.

"He accused me of going behind his back and cheating on him. "You women are a dirty lot of dirty b****es," he accused me. He said, "A man can' trust you even while he's at work." "

"Oh, you poor, poor thing…"

"…So he had the idea of how he would "satisfy" me." She began to cry again and Sylvia left her to collect herself. "When I began to scream he stuffed his underpants into my mouth. Imagine that. Just think of it! I wriggled around so he would not put that thing in my mouth then he had a bright idea... a sick idea... he tied my hands behind my back with my bra... my bra, Sylvie." She was quiet again and the tears flowed once more. "Then...then...when I was helpless... oh, Sylvie. I can't explain the pain... the humiliation. My husband! My worst enemy! He went on and on...I don't know why I didn't die. I know I have internal injuries. I am in so much pain, you can't imagine.

"When the children left for school, he was still here. He din' allow them to come into the room. He left after them without looking in and I was glad about that. But when he's sober, he won't do anything. I know it makes him feel bad so he stays drunk to not face reality."

Sylvia completed the bed making then gently helped Elizabeth to the shower. "Before we leave, Elizabeth, there's something I need to throw into the dam down yonder." She took a plastic bag from the kitchen, and added a large stone to it with Taylor's gadget. Good. Now it'd sink to the bottom of the dam and stay there.

They soon left, thanks to a nanny who loaned Sylvia her car.

At the crowded clinic they heard about the increasing problem of wife abuse. Gasps of shock and horror from the other patients soon had her story out. They shared stories of their own experiences. One woman told of a friend who was jailed for killing her husband who was coming at her with a bush knife. She shot him with his own gun.

Another burst out with her own story of how she got a group of her girl friend to waylay her husband and give him a good doing up. They were masked and made it clear he was being given a woman-hiding, "just for the fun of it". That brought on a loud laugh.

"Did it work?" someone wanted to know.

"Of course. He got home so sore and battered and bruised and I tried hard to hide my smile. I treated him like my poor, poor child who was in a meeting with the school bully." Laughter.

The men in the seated queues shuffled their feet, cleared their throats and looked badly out of place. One by one they rose to their feet with a muttered, "I need a smoke." and "Me, too."

Three Evangelists walked into the room carrying Bibles. One of them began a scriptural song and the patients joined in, singing softly and sweetly. Business at the desk continued while the singing proceeded.

The oldest of the Evangelists held up a hand and the singing eased off. He cleared his throat and greeted everyone present. His mates translated into Zulu and Afrikaans. He then preached the gospel of God's grace and mercy. Most of the patients responded in their own tongue.

"It's like that, Preacher."

"Preach it, man of God!"

"Amen."

"Hallelujah."

Most people just sat there and listened.

Eventually they thanked the people for listening and told them to join a Bible-teaching church so they could get to know the Saviour God had sent the world.

Much talk broke out after they had left. They discussed the truth of what they'd heard and one or two made daring dismissive statements.

"Religious nuts! Don't listen to them; they'll fill your heads with a lot of nonsense."

"Jesus is coming, my foot! He's been coming for centuries. Has He come? No! And I don't believe He will…ever!

"Hey," one man cried passionately", jumping to his feet. "Do you even believe there ees a god? Look at the world around you? If there were a god donchu think he was gonna clean up all this mess… this cruelty? Even chu'ren are being raped and some in their own homes. Look at that woman there…" pointing at Elizabeth. "If I was god, I was gonna strike him with lightning there and then. Dead in front of her an' her chu'ren." Sheepishly he flopped down and immediately jumped up again. "Smoke break." He trotted out without looking back.

Reactions from the crowd differed. While the opinions were being hotly debated, Elizabeth's name came up. Laboriously she got up with Sylvia's help. Sounds of sympathy and opinions of what that monster-husband's just deserts would be, followed them. There was silence while Elizabeth was tended.

Then they heard that the mortuary had seen far worse cases.

"De Vee…de Vee…what are you to Taylor de Vee?" the nurse in attendance wanted to know.

Elizabeth and Sylvia answered simultaneously. "He's my husband." "It's her husband."

Gasps from behind.

"Taylor's wife!"

"The dirty dog!"

"No! Such a good man!"

"I don' believe it."

"Taylor's wife," the nurse nudged her colleague and indicated with her head, "over here."

17

"Huh?" Clearly, she was shocked. "His wife?"

"Believe it," she muttered in Afrikaans. The fact that Sylvia and Elizabeth understood every word mattered not a jot to her. Her stage whisper held everyone spellbound. Those near the back crept down the side isles to get closer. One woman acted as interpreter for the curious non-Afrikaans speakers.

"He always talks about what a mean piece of work she is. Looks like he lost it. Good for him. Serves her right. She'll come right. *Jisslaaik*! Just look at her. He overdid it a bit, but…"

Her friend chipped in also in Afrikaans, "No, let her suffer. Too long he's been putting up with her s**t. Look at that mouth… now it will only open at the right time." They giggled cruelly, peeping at her from under their false eyelashes and painted eyelids.

Meanwhile the enrapt listeners showed their disgust but quietly continued listening. They weren't going to miss a word!

The unsympathetic nurse looked coldly at Elizabeth. "We know Taylor. He's a good man an' he told us all about your wicked ways. Stop being his problem…"

Sylvia exploded. "How dare you…"

"It takes two to tango," the nurse sneered at her. Elizabeth's stricken demeanour shut Sylvia up. The nurse hadn't finished. "For your information, we have treated Taylor for 'dirty sickness' and where did he get it?" Dramatically she pointed an accusing finger at the suffering woman. Elizabeth straightened up and gasped. Then she doubled up with pain. Sylvia gathered her into her arms. She looked coldly at the outspoken nurse.

"See to his abused wife so we can go from here. She happens to be here for her healing not to be further abused by you. I wonder what your superiors will think of your behaviour towards an ailing woman. The other patients have taken in all you've been saying. There must be people in this crowd who know this woman and her wonder-boy husband. They may tell you a thing or two about him. And the nurses' hostel at this hospital is commonly known as "the cake box". I wonder why."

Giggles from the audience and mutters of "the cake box – die koek blik" in Afrikaans. Interpretations for Zulu speakers who related their stories and names for the notorious hostel and its inmates.

Sylvia continued. "Pity the nurses are all painted with that brush. You have been filled with the lies of a dirty, rotten monster, and you choose to believe them. Good for you. May be a good idea if he divorced her and married you! Maybe he'll change and creep back to her with dirty lies about you!" The stunned nurses listened wordlessly, perhaps regretting their foolish, unprofessional outspokenness.

X-rays showed that Elizabeth had nothing broken or torn but the bruises received attention.

When they got back from the clinic and the police station, she put Elizabeth to bed. Although a complaint was registered, no case was made. The police called it a domestic affair and refused to do any more.

Taylor's friends in different places cleaned up after him with no thought to the welfare of his victims… his wife and children.

Sylvia was too ashamed to tell Jordan about their visit to the hospital and Elizabeth's injuries. "How can I tell him about such intimate things about another woman? It'll hurt her dignity," she reasoned to herself. She could not expose Elizabeth's extremely embarrassing experience. Enough that those cold-hearted medical staff members and lawmen knew! If the township grapevine was as efficient as it was reputed to be, then sooner or later they'd hear anyway. Taylor frequently visited his shebeen-owner brother there.

She'd told everyone Elizabeth was home with 'flu while she was recovering from the worst of the agonising pain.

The children knew that it was not well with the de Vee household. They had no idea their mother knew all about it. Sonja let the cat out of the bag at dinner one evening much to the annoyance of her siblings.

"Sonja, shut up!" Olivia was mortified. They were sworn to secrecy by the emotionally ragged de Vee children.

"Why should she shut up? What was that again, Sonja?" Sylvia's ears pricked up sharply. Jordan stiffened.

"I forgot," Sonja mumbled, looking down at her plate. "I'm full, Mama, can I go to my room?"

"No, sweetheart, we want to know more about what you were saying."

"I can't," she wailed, "Cora said we mustn't talk about it to grown-ups." Then she became highly agitated. "Daddy, will you do those awful things to Mama, too?'

Jordan got up from his seat and gathered his little blossom into his arms. "Oh, no love, no. Are you sure Cora was being truthful? That doesn't sound like Taylor; he's so jolly all the time."

"That's what you choose to think," Sylvia burst out quite spontaneously. She could have bitten her tongue out, but it was too late. Finally, the whole sorry saga came out.

Jordan sounded angry when they discussed it later in bed. "I suppose I was being an ostrich – putting my head in the sand. I didn't want to believe this is happening right under our noses. A filthy blast from the past we were running away from. I pretended and pretended but those dark lumps on her face…they're not natural, are they? They're here one day, gone the next and then the lumps seem to get lumps…"

"Those are courtesy of her dearly beloved who has threatened her life should she disgrace or dishonour him by leaving him!" Sylvia said curtly. And you don't know the half of it, she said to herself.

"Dishonour! Looks like he's done that all by himself! What about the promises he made when they got married…the skunk! I *will* bring up the subject. I don't know how, but I'll look for the opportunity."

"Just don't make things worse for Elizabeth. She doesn't know Cora has spoken to our girls."

He was quiet for a moment. "Now I understand the need for a walking stick. What a monster! I feel like going to squelch his scrawny neck like a cool drink can… right now… this very minute."

Sylvia had a time trying to soothe the agitated man.

One evening Jordan and Taylor were at Perry's as usual where Taylor had his usual stout and a triple shot of vodka, "just to wash away the day's dust," before going home. Jordan had his usual lemon and lime with lemonade, mint and lots of ice.

21

"How's things between you and Elizabeth, Teeza?"

"Huh?" Taylor almost choked. "Why you wanna know, Jors, my man? Did she choon something?"

"No, she didn't say anything; I'm just asking. Families often have hidden problems. And you know what they say about a problem shared."

"You wanna share my problems, Jors? There's some nice nurses I know…"

"Hey! Forget that! For better… for worse, remember?"

"Me an Liz is jus' great but you know how it goes, a man can' live on mutton only." He flashed his toothless grin and winked lewdly. Jordan shrank back in disgust.

"Don't talk dirty. You and Elizabeth are the ideal couple."

"You think so, ou Jors? But you know women – can't trust 'em far's you can kick 'em…"

"Says the man who needs more than mutton…"

Taylor threw back his head and guffawed… loudly…beery spit flying.

Trying to hide his disgust, Jordan wiped his face with his sleeve. This made Taylor laugh even louder. "I mus' say it don' spray it, hey, Jors? Sorry 'bout that," he spluttered, holding a hand in front of his mouth.

"For your information, Tees, Sylvia is the only woman I have ever slept with and she will be the only one… ever!"

Taylor's eyes opened wide. He burst out laughing, eyes fixed on Jordan. Then he jumped up onto the counter top and shouted, "Hoooo…everyone…listen here…" Jordan grabbed him by the legs, pulled him down roughly, caught him around the throat and held him close up. Taylor's eyes bulged. "If I ever... *ever* hear that you made fun of my relationship with my wife behind my back, I'll slaughter you!"

The shocked man became quite docile. He daren't pit his muscles against those of this large man. Jordan cooled down as suddenly as he'd flared up.

"Sorry, Tees. I reacted without thinking. My family is my treasure. Don't go there."

"I am the sorry fool, ou Jors. I din mean it. But if you din stop me, maybe I was... No hard feelings, ou maat?"

"No hard feelings, mate."

So... the man was into adultery.

"An' that's his problem," Jordan told Sylvia later that night. Sylvia nodded. Then she related a bit of the incident at the hospital with the uncaring nurse.

"Makes sense. She was taken aback when she heard Taylor has a wife. Bet she gave him a flea in his ear. But there's more to it, Jordy, you mark my words. That toothless wonder has psychological problems and he needs to see a psychiatrist."

Jordan laughed heartily. "Toothless wonder, hey? To heck with him and his problems. Right now, I have my wife in my arms and she's discussing another man!" Mock angrily, "Woman! Where's my respect?" and he drew her tightly to him.

Family life for the Madden's was as blissful as it was ghastly for the de Vees. As a family they epitomized misery, depression, despondency and just plain old unhappiness. Elizabeth was like an automaton. She jerked violently when touched unexpectedly. Her laughter was high pitched and forced. Her smile never reached her eyes. She was a bundle of nerves. Sylvia had to pull her up on several occasions for snapping at the children.

Sidney showed definite signs of fear and misery: he was crabby and wet the bed almost every night and his father punished him severely every time. He did not allow Elizabeth to wake him up at night to take him to the bathroom because, he bellowed, that boy is old enough to get up when his bladder is full! "What son of mine is this? Is he going to become a man, p***ing the bed day after day? Hey? Tell me that! You baby him too much. He must grow up!"

"Be reasonable, Taylor, the boy may be nervy because of the constant shouting, swearing and fighting in this house…"

"And whose fault is that? If you weren't such a stupid woman there'd, be peace in this house. I blame you! You! And don't look at me like that! I feel like planting one in your ugly face right now!" He advanced on her threateningly.

"Taylor, please, man. Don't upset the children again."

"And it'll be your fault. You disrespectful thing, you! Answering me back like that…" he caught sight of a tear-drenched Sidney cowering beside his mother, hanging onto her sleeve, thumb in mouth.

"That snivelling thing hanging on to you like a scared puppy…Come here, you… mummy's boy… you wanna suck tietie?"

"No, Pa," the boy yelled as his dad yanked him and dragged him screaming to the kitchen. The sound of the wooden spoon and her son's pitiful yells had Elizabeth in tears which she hastily tried to control. "Now get out of here and go water the vegetable garden."

"Taylor!" Liz shouted, "It's too cold outside for a little boy to be watering the garden without something warm on. And it's my garden; I prefer to water it myself." He frogmarched the boy out and soon returned.

"Don't you tell me how to handle my son. It's through you he's a moffie! A moffie! My son! Not a *him*! A *shim*!" The hysterical man was banging his chest. "You ruined my boys, woman!! De Vee boys…crying and wetting the bed! And this one needs to toughen up. Let him water the garden. When I was his age…huh! Don't let me start on that…"

Suddenly he turned on his heel, walked to their bedroom and soon he was out the door, and off in his ramshackle car – successor to the ramshackle van that had long since exhaled its last funky cloud of vicious fumes.

She rushed out to help Sidney. He was weeping bitterly, his teeth were chattering, and his whole body was vibrating with cold. He was wet from head to toe because the wind whipped the water from the nozzle right back onto him. "My baby," she cried, taking the hose from him, closing the tap and gathering him in her arms. She rushed him to the bath for a warm soaking.

For Sidney it was too late; by evening he had a raging temperature. There was no sign of Taylor…what was she to do? Fearing that any delay could prove fatal, she wrapped Sidney up warmly, strapped Cohen onto her back, praying he'd stay there, and gathered up the sick child in her arms.

"Please take care of Cora," she whispered hoarsely.

An hour later he was in the Intensive Care Unit of the local hospital. Jordan and Sylvia were fuming! "If I could get my hands around his throat! Huh! I'd squeeze until he went limp."

"And I'd be right there beside you, banging his back with my sharpest heel." Both realised they had no recourse to any measures on his family's behalf. It was entirely up to Elizabeth to up and out, and call his bluff. "Surely, he won't kill her. Jordan, what do you think?"

"I can't think pass this thing right now, Syl."

"What about the children? They'd be orphaned and he'd be in jail, wouldn't he? Such lovely children... please let there still be a Sidney tomorrow."

Cora was left fast asleep and Olivia and Kay'd been sent off to babysit the sleeping girl.

Elizabeth soon came out to speak to them.

"Please take Cohen with you; I'm going to spend the night here with Sidney. The doc feels he may last the night if all goes well...if he's lucky!" She was trying her best to keep a stiff upper lip. "Luck! I never got my share in this life... only Taylor! All I got is Taylor!" She began to cry and to shout and to scream. She was hysterical. A nurse came running, took in the scene and forcefully led her away. "She needs a tranquilliser," she hissed. "I'll take her back to Doctor Bussey."

Sylvia and Jordan were not quite sure what to do. Cohen was beginning to fuss after the shock of seeing his mother's outburst. He cried out, straining to get to his mother, "Mama...Mama... wanna go to Mama."

"Hush, Cohen, Mama's coming now-now," Sylvia was weeping into his blanket. Jordan took the boy, hurled him onto his shoulders and soon Jordan was playing horsey-horsey with him and the boy was giggling crazily for more. Before long the nurse reappeared. "She's alright ... she's in good hands. You take the boy home with you, please. Where is her husband? Is she a single mom, do you know?"

"Of course, we know; they are our neighbours. Her husband is where all husbands who are not at home at this time of the day go." There was venom in Sylvia's voice; her narrowed eyes flashed fire. The nurse nodded her head. This kind of problem was certainly not new to them.

When they got home Cohen began to fret again. The sound of Taylor's car trundling home alerted them. "There's Daddy," Sylvia thought she'd pacify the boy. He grabbed her with both hands, digging his little fingers into her shoulders and shutting his eyes tight. His whole body began to shudder. Then he let out a strange cry, low pitched and hair-raising. No child should react to their father like that! Even her father had not had this extreme effect on them. Taylor deserved to be hanged! Jordan went out to meet him.

Worrisome was the fact that the boy had reverted into babyhood. "Okay, okay, Cohen. You'll not go to Daddy. You'll stay right here with Aunty Sylvie an Andy, and Luke, and Sonja...an..." Luke appeared in the doorway, rubbing his eyes and yawning widely, "Cohen!" his cry of delight was genuine. "Come to Lukie." He took the boy from his mother and made to return to his room but stopped at the door. "What gives, Mama?" he asked, turning around. "Where's Sidney?"

"Sidney's in hospital. They suspect double pneumonia..."

"Is that bad?"

"Can be but we think Aunty Elizabeth took him in on time. He should be okay in no time flat."

"That's okay, then." He walked out with the excited toddler tweaking his ears as he blew loudly into his little stomach. The boy chuckled delightedly.

Soon Jordan walked in with Taylor hot on his heels.

He slurred drunkenly at Sylvia who gazed at him like he was a fly in her milkshake. He did not wait for her to say anything but burst out with: "Youse think youse are better... Cohen! Elizabeth!" he screamed, "Come out here before I come fetch you. Sidney! Cora! Come out! Now!"

In the boys' bedroom Cohen dived under Luke's bed and lay there quivering, little teeth chattering in absolute terror. The hollow sound that accompanied the chattering tore at the very fabric of Luke's being. No little boy should fear his father like this! A boldness came over him and he stomped into the lounge.

Before his parents could stop him, he shouted at Taylor: "Go to the hospital, Mr de Vee, your son, Sidney, is there and if he's lucky he'll live." He stared at the man in total disgust. "I'm glad you're not my father!" Jordan and Sylvia cried out simultaneously: "Luke!" A rebellious Luke stood his ground. "I am, too... glad. But I'm not s'pose to be rude to adults but I'm not sorry I said that." he turned and ran out the door.

"I can see what that dirty b**** has done...she put everyone against me..."

"No, Taylor, you did that all by yourself," Sylvia snapped at him. "You've no need for help there!"

28

"You think you who... Mrs Some...Body? Well let me tell you this, Mrs Some... Body...that highty-tighty husband of yours has a b**** in town. Arks him... go on, arks him. Arks him now," pointing a wobbly finger, "There he is... go on, arks him. He tole me with his own mouth..." he ground out between hiccups.

"I'm asking him nothing. Go home and sleep it off..."

"Sleep what off? You think you better'n me? You take my family away soon as my back is turned... there was nutting wrong wif Sidney when I lef' home... nutting, you hear me? I know they right in this house jus' to try me... I'm ginne donner that woman good an' proper..."

"You will donner no one, Taylor." Jordan finally spoke up. "As long as you are living on my property, your donnering days are OVER! I'm glad I heard it from your mouth... now I can take action.'

"Ac-sin? Ac-sin? You unner petticoat guv'ment an' you wanna tell me that b*** s***. Come, I'll show you, you moffie." He was frothing at the mouth. Jordan dive-tackled him, slung him over his shoulder and carried him yelling and screaming the worst obscenities they hadn't even heard in their childhood homes.

By this time the children were all up. Jordan gave the twisting, squirming, shouting man a cold shower under the outside tap at his home and shoved him through the open lounge window. He landed on the sofa under the window and rolled off onto the tiled floor, with a loud thud. "Ouch!" Jordan muttered, flinching, "that was his head – knock some sense into him." Aloud he called out: "Take yerself t' bed, Taylor. I hope you get pneumonia and land in hospital in the ICU next to yer son."

A shocked Kay appeared, closely followed by Olivia and Cora, shouting, "Dad, wait." Jordan slapped his forehead. "Come out at once, you girls. I'd forgotten. Elizabeth won't be home tonight." The writhing man on the floor was too dazed to do or say anything right then.

"Arks him… go on, arks him. Arks him now." Sylvia giggled. "What should I arks you, dearly beloved?"

"Taylor's drunken talk. I've no intention of being an adulterer. No deliberate wrongdoing from this ole sinner."

One day Jordan and Taylor had a heart-to-heart. Jordan came straight to the point and Taylor was caught unawares.

"You got me there, ou Jors. I hate what I do but I jus' can' help it. When I see Elizabeth, my fists ball up…"

"Have you thought of seeing a psychiatrist? Stop seeing other women? Would you say your life is going great guns? Is this the life you dreamed of having? Is this the life you'll tell your grandchildren about one day? Maybe you have childhood issues you have to get out of your system…"

"Lotta questions, ou Jors. You don' wanna know 'bout my chile'ood; let's don' go there, ou pal. My chile'ood was one long nightmare, till I gave my father rat poison."

"You WHAT?" Jordan exploded. "You know the saying, what goes around comes around? What if your children do that to you? Will your system take it? You want your children to become father killers?"

30

"I hear whatchu saying, but the old man din die, ou Jors. He was very sick for a long time an' his stomick never come right. When he did die it was in a taxi accident. He was coming from the clinic… hey, maybe I did kill him… he went once every fortnight for stomach treatment. Up to today no one knows what I done…only you…"

Taylor began to cry. "Help me, ou Jors!" he was sobbing wildly. Jordan found crumpled, greasy tissues in the console which he handed to the man.

That conversation made Taylor so mad at himself for showing his weakness, he turned the screws even tighter on his family. He locked Elizabeth in, leaving her bewildered, needing to go to work. When he got home, he thrashed her soundly because "you are a dirty b****; how'd I know you din have men in here while I was working my ar** off to put food into that big mouth o' yours? Huh?" His children who spent the afternoon with the Madden's ran home when he arrived, only to find their mother in a state.

Cohen and Sidney reported him to Jordan who took it up with Taylor. Trying to reason with the man, Jordan finally convinced him that she was not doing the things he was doing. Taylor actually looked shamefaced, "You right, ou Jors, you right, you right."

He proved to be creative however, thinking up other ways of expressing the evil that lurked within. He made life unbearable not just for Elizabeth but for the children as well. Often "Monster Dad" came home after ten and capsized the whole family. He'd whip the children out of their beds and chase them all out of the house. "Go to the Madden's… go… go… you'll all burn inside there…just you wait n see." Elizabeth learned how to slip out while he was whipping the children so that by the time he thought they were alone and he could abuse her at will, she had gone. The frustrated man would eventually pass out, exhausted from screaming for Elizabeth, and shouting the direst threats.

As time went by the Madden and the beleaguered de Vee children became more like siblings than just friends. Very little changed as the years went by. Taylor continued to abuse his family, and his children's ire grew with the years. They hated him with passion and often begged their mother to divorce him. They lived with her explanation and just hoped that in time he would change, or die. Sidney and Cohen often discussed what they would do when they were big enough.

"Till death do us part," Elizabeth explained to them on one occasion when they had another Daddy discussion.

"Well, Ma, it looks like you'll get that from the one you made that promise with. If Da' doesn't kill you one day, I dinno…you'll have a heart attack or something."

"Or we may just do the job," Cohen mumbled. "I'm tired of this life… sick n tired."

Much to the shocked surprise of his family, Taylor actually came home one night and declared he was sick n tired of drinking. Those words made Cohen wonder if his father was a mind reader. He made a show of apologising to his family for his behaviour. "If I have behaved badly towards any of you, then I apologise. From the bottom of my heart, I apologise. Taylor de Vee is a new man." And indeed, things did change. Long enough for the children to relax.

Unbeknown to them he had experienced great pain and consulted a doctor. The doctor made a diagnosis that startled him. His spleen could take no more abuse and his liver was badly endangered. The damage was great but could be arrested if he stopped drinking and went on the prescribed treatment. Taylor kept the treatment a secret, but he could not hide his soberness.

Elizabeth told Sylvia about Taylor's welcome announcement. "From the bottom of his heart he is sorry," Elizabeth did not sound convinced at all.

"From the heart of his bottom, more likely! I just hope he's serious." Sylvia couldn't hide her distrust. Elizabeth repeated Sylvia's words – *the heart of his bottom, hey?* and they giggled like schoolgirls. "The images!" laughed Elizabeth.

Then Taylor had promotion at work. It meant a considerably increased salary. Being sober for so long, his superiors, who included Jordan, decided it was time to reward his hard work and his excellent skills. He was elated.

And so was his wife. She hoped that promotion would make a better man of him… keep him from ever going back to his old ways.

Taylor was on top of the world. Finally, he had the position he had long been after. He was told repeatedly that drinking and absenteeism were held against him. "Absenteeism?" exclaimed a shocked Elizabeth when she heard that. "He has never stayed home from work no matter how vile he's feeling the following day." She dared not ask him about it. She knew about the "Cow Shed" – a girls' hostel so named for a good reason, talk told, where many husbands spent much of their time and money... where money turned even a bloated old man into the ladies' man.

The "Cake Tin" scandal had resulted in Taylor going elsewhere to play the field. The grape vine broadcast let it be known that the nurses were more shocked by Elizabeth's appearance than they let on. They wanted nothing more to do with him or his generosity with alcohol and good times. He left the Cake Tin with spit on his head and face and a long-kept, 'ripe' bed pan emptied over his head.

Thankfully those days were behind them now.

Elizabeth was experiencing the early days of her marriage once again. Taylor was attentive; he never alluded to the past and nor did she. The children, suspicious and very cautious at first, were at peace and when he got in from work, they showed genuine excitement. Elizabeth often pinched herself to make sure this was the real deal! She would not admit to anyone that deep inside she waited with bated breath for her bubble to burst. When he got in sober each night, she let up a silent prayer of gratitude. "I'll never tell a soul this but I really hate this man. I deserve the highest prize for my excellent acting."

Taylor's workmates planned a celebration, township style! The Madden's and the de Vee's went off to the township where the party was being held. Taylor and Elizabeth were guests of honour. They sat at the beautifully appointed main table along with the Madden's and the excited outgoing foreman, who was eagerly looking forward to his retirement.

The speeches consisted of entertaining Taylor stories that had the guests in stitches. Taylor's childhood friends roasted him! One after the other they came up to tell how Taylor, a naughty little instigator in his childhood, led them into all sorts of escapades. His children laughed the loudest of all.

It was a jolly party. Delicious aromas filled the air. The spread of stews and curries with rice, pap (polenta), and salads of every description made a colourful, tempting display. The guests enthused over the amazing standard of the party. There was so much meat to eat, and the meat lovers went to town! There was spit roast lamb, large Texan steaks, spatchcocked chickens, and they even had an array of sea creatures: huge prawns, lobsters, crabs and one very large fish. "All the way from Mozambique," they were informed. Sylvia shuddered at the sight of the crustaceans. "People eat those?" she whispered in Jordan's ear. "I thought people only eat fish from the sea."

"You got a lot to learn, sweetness," he laughed. "Try them. You may just like them."

"I don't think so. Crabs? Nope! And not even those others, thank you very much. There's lots of tempting dishes. I'll go for those."

The drinks table groaned under the sheer weight of the number of bottles it carried. A very large galvanised bath alongside held huge ice blocks with a surprisingly large variety of beers crammed into it. Amongst the beer bottles was an assortment of soft drinks as well.

The crowd had a whale of a time! They were all in high spirits. Taylor danced with his wife a lot. Even the children got into it. Jordan and Sylvia soon took to the floor as well and Sylvia really let her hair down. They danced with their children. They danced with strangers. They enjoyed the night immensely.

They all left at dawn, exhausted, happy and singing rowdily.

It could be said without fear of contradiction that a good time was had by all.

One night, soon thereafter, something happened that changed Jordan's life forever.

Part 2
Beware the Little Foxes that Destroy the Vine

During the week following his promotion celebration, Taylor became quiet and withdrawn, almost morose. When Friday came, Taylor gave Sidney a hastily scribbled note to give to Jordan on his way to the school bus. Sidney was a strapping thirteen-year-old. The boys were ardent rugby players and it showed. The note was brief, "Perry's after work."

Sidney pushed the note under the door with a shout, "JAMES, NOTE UNDER THE DOOR FOR YOUR DA'." He had a bad feeling but brushed it aside telling himself that he must be positive. It could be that his dad needed to confide in another man. Maybe he was having hassles at work in his new position? Maybe he had other problems that made him so depressed lately? He shrugged his shoulders and joined his siblings.

When Jordan got the note, he looked a little worried. Perry's was the pub. They stopped popping in after work when Taylor got on the wagon. By the time he left work Taylor had already gone. He was really tired but he thought he'd go see what the man had to say. Taylor was already there. That was his back-pack, his tall glass of stout, and alongside was what looked like his lemon and lime drink.

"So...the man's decided to fall off the wagon! That party ... all that liquor must've got to him...and he not having a taste of it." Jordan was worried. But the sight of the unmistakable lemon and lime drink cheered him.

"Nice guy," he smiled appreciatively, "Cheers, mate; bless your backslidden heart." With a thankful whoop he grabbed it and drank thirstily then realised it tasted different...it contained alcohol! The very instant the realisation hit him he heard the frantic shout: JORDAN! WAIT! It was Taylor shouting from the Men's room door.

Too late!

He'd taken his first alcoholic drink!

The glass was not meant for him.

The alcoholic warmth quickly spread through him, making him feel alive...dissipating the feeling of tiredness! His shoulders felt relaxed, his head felt floaty, and he'd just had a mouthful! He looked back at Taylor, smiled, stretched his glass towards Taylor then swiftly swallowed the rest of the drink.

"Grrrr," he roared, shaking his head vigorously. "What was that? It's doing good things to my whole body."

Taylor's intention was to try Jordan's favourite with "a little extra something". He took in Jordan's mistake at a glance but it was too late to stop him. Jordan shook his whole body like a water-drenched animal shaking itself. "Grr!" he gritted out again, "I feel so good, better'n James Brown."

Taylor laughed out loud and sang the line from the song. Slapping his friend on the back, he said, "Welcome to manhood, pal. Here, WAITRESS... you gotta have another shot, ou pal. If one is good, two is better and three is best..."

As it turned out Taylor had to stop Jordan... hold it, my china... steady, ole boy .... not so much so soon. But Jordan wasn't having any. One after the other he downed his favourite lemon and lime drinks only this time with vodka added.

"Taylor, you sly ole fox…" he slurred, head bobbing drunkenly. "Why din you tell me it was so good? Man-o-man. I feel great."

"I tried to explain, ou Jors, my man, but you wouldn' listen. Whatchu think, why does the manne comes to the pub so often? Home is jis' not the same."

"You got that right," Jordan slurred drunkenly. Suddenly he bent over sprayed the whole area a nasty, smelly, messy, goopy, slimy layer of stuff! It sent those close by scattering with shrieks of disgust and horror.

As Taylor helped him out, there were calls from within:

"Leave the drinking to the men, Jordy–boy."

"Teach him better, ou Teeza. You know the ropes."

Taylor took his friend home, leaving Jordan's van in the pub backyard.

When he got home Sylvia took one look and threw up her arms. Her horrified scream brought the children running. They stared open-mouthed. Luke was the first to laugh; only it sounded more like a scornful snicker. Sylvia scowled at him but it was too late – it caught on. Soon they were all in fits of laughter. Their dad was a frightful sight! The 'matter' was all down his shirt front, his hair had a share of it too and his eyes bulged like little eggs.

"'lo, fam'ly," he managed and slid out of Taylor's hold. He passed out on the floor. Between Taylor and Sylvia, he was soon bathed, with great difficulty judging from Sylvia's frequent outbursts and Taylor's patient encouragement.

"Sylvie, it ok; it ok, Sylvie, he be awright now-now Sylvie."

"Sylvie, don' worry; tomorrow he be right as rain."

"It were a mistake, Sylvie … gen'win."

This ingratiating man, who had fallen off the wagon… again…. was being intensely annoying. Sylvia gritted her teeth. At the back of her mind, she was seeing his poor, unfortunate family.

The following day Jordan was deeply remorseful. He apologised over and over to his family. He did not let up that inside he was not apologetic at all. On the contrary, he wanted a repeat performance! Badly! Who would have thought it? Only he'd go easy on it. No more over-doing it. No wonder Taylor…

Perish the thought! He would not… could not… condone Taylor's behaviour under any circumstance. Wife battering? Family violence? He shuddered deeply as a flash of childhood memory washed over him. Surely a good drink should make you happy – not belligerent. His mind was pretty busy. He felt happy last night… until he couldn't remember any more… except for the throwing up… What a disgrace! He'd have to apologise to Perry and the men. And Perry's cleaning lady… she must be fuming, he thought. He'd get her a thank you/ pardon me gift next pay day.

Turned out Jordan was an instant alcoholic. Just that one time and his body shouted out for more. It clawed at his mind; it squeezed his insides; the desire for more dominated his thoughts. He couldn't wait for the work day to end and each day he would torment himself, pass the pub very slowly and reluctantly go home. "Whatchu think, why does the manne comes to the pub so often? Home is jis' not the same." Taylor's words constantly came back to torment him even more.

Jordan staggered in blind drunk one night two weeks later, defensive and downright belligerent! Sylvia plonked his supper in front of him in a huff and it annoyed him vastly! He jumped to his feet, holding onto the table and back-handed her across the face. Blood spurted from her nose! Hearing the commotion, the children came running. Jordan was staring at her, head weaving to and fro, unsteadily holding onto the table.

James noticed the bulge in Jordan's jacket pocket. It matched Taylor's. James was aghast! What was starting? Where would it end? "Taylor!" the name passed through his mind in a flash. "Is Dad on the same path?" There stood his mother, nose bloodied, staring at this fiendish stranger as though hypnotised. Sonja jumped wildly at her dad, clung to him and sank her teeth into his behind. She bit with all her might and he turned sharply to ward her off. The unsteady man keeled over and went sprawling, chair and all, with Sonja narrowly missing falling under him. James made an involuntary grab that saved her.

The screaming and shouting was exactly like it was at the de Vees.

That was the start of a whole new life for the Madden household. It was as the saying goes: he who'd been socialising with the dogs came alive with fleas.

Sylvia drooped visibly. She became an abused wife. Clearly attack was Jordan's defence tactic. She never said anything bad about Jordan to their children; instead she made excuses for him. They heard them all.

"He's still your dad inside. This is just a phase; it will pass, you'll see"

"I refuse to give up on him. He's a good man, really. You all know that."

"The man I married and lived with all these years is inside there – he will come back...soon, I just know it."

No one mentioned a word when the plaque on the gate disappeared.

The Madden had tumbled from his pedestal.

They were in the pub again. Together. Wonder of wonderful wonders. They were drinking companions now. Real buddies. And they had a lot of catching up to do. Taylor was like a little boy who had taken Father Christmas home with his entire company and his entire load. He laughed too much, drank too much, spoke out of turn too much, and ignored the complainers.

"Taylor! I do not need to know what happens in your dratted bedroom. Shut your toothless face!"

"Stop with the filth! Your mouth is a proper sewerage pipe!"

"Jordan! Shut that man up, please."

"Hey, Taylor, here... put my holey, stinky sock in it!"

The appeals came in crude form. Taylor laughed so much he fell off his stool. Someone picked him up like a sack of cement and plonked him outside on the steps. "Stay there!" the man shouted, pointing a threatening finger at him.

Perry, the owner-barman yelled, "Hey, that's my customer. If you don't like his stupidity, you get out! We all know Teeza suffers from giddurexia ain't that right, Jordy-boy?"

"What? Can you say that word again?" someone shouted, amazed. Jordan stared at him blankly.

The patrons and regulars of Perry's were in fits of laughter trying to repeat the word. "Go on, Perry, shay it agen," Jordan squinted at him, grinning foolishly yet annoyed that his friend was so badly treated.

"Gid-du-rex-ee-u… giddurexia… giddurexia. Old word. You pipsqueaks were still hanging from the trees by your tails. I can even spell it." He said slowly, his grin pure mischief.

"Go on, this ain't school, no need for spelling… jus' tell us what it means," someone called out, while Jordan battled to get his sloppy-drunk, angry, humiliated friend back inside. Soon he was seated again, his head lolling loosely from side to side. Jordan just about managed to remain on his feet though he staggered and stumbled, bumping into everything and everyone he passed.

"One more drink, Jordy-boy and your cycle will be complete," Perry called out. Then he addressed the room. "You really, really want to know what it means?"

Shouts of assent, jeers and hoots of derision. "Just a made up word," someone shouted loudly at him.

"This white man thinks we fools," someone else called out.

"Hey, Perry, you think we bruin-ous is schoopit?"

"He thinks we schoopit, I bet!"

"Okay, okay, hold your horses and cool your coolers; I'll tell you. It's a rather nasty condition where there's a continuous flow from the colon to the brain." He used his hands to demonstrate the path of the flow.

Unruly laughter, crude opinions and ribald expressions of agreement exploded. The place was in uproar! Confusion confounded! Some in more advanced stages of drunkenness landed on the floor and across the plush, cigarette-burn pocked burgundy imitation leather built-in perimeter couches, unable to keep control of their senses or their bodily functions. And this compounded the situation.

Screams of

"Sies!"

"Yuck!"

"Go to de toilet, and sh** there!"

"E-e-e-e-u! The toothless one screamed!"

One of the men took out a box of matches and walked around striking match after match and waving it in the air to eliminate the dreadful pong, all the while loudly grumbling about the manners of some people.

Perry spoke up: "Hey, manne... whoever let off like that, something died in your guts long time ago. It is rotten! Go to the hossie and have it out!" Laughter and cries of, *not me, Perry*.

Finally the laughter died down and some form of order was restore. Then one old biddy muttered, "From colon to brain, hey? One way!" He drew out 'one' comically, on his knees, head on the floor, wildly wiggling an index finger above his head. His muffled laugh sounded more like the whistle of a train racing through a tunnel.

There is a saying, 'the devil looks after his own'. There is every likelihood that saying was proven that night. Jordan managed to drive as far as the gate and that is where they spent the night.

Very early in the morning Jordan awoke with a loud groan. "Oo-oo-oo," he moaned piteously. "My head. Taylor!" He shook the man heartlessly. "Taylor, wake up." The snoring man had to be forcefully awakened. When finally he opened his eyes, he too met the day with a loud groan of real pain. Looking at each other, they began to laugh holding their tortured heads.

"Where are we? Oh." Taylor sat up and looked around. Then he looked at his companion and began to laugh doing his throbbing head further damage.

"Whatchu laughing at?" Jordan squinted at him out of one eye.

"A-chu, my china. You so ugly, you'll frighten the children." He doubled over, laughing and groaning and moaning. "Oo…my head, my head."

Jordan turned the rear-view mirror and gave a squeal of horror. "Tjo! I look almost ugly as you, ou Tees." Then he, too went into waves of painful laughter. Finally he slapped Taylor on the back and nodded towards the gate. "Open up, ou maat."

Sheepish they went home to families whose collective nerves were at breaking point. Both Jordan and Taylor decided to play the silence game. Sylvia kept out of Jordan's way while he lumbered and lurched around readying himself to go out again.

Meanwhile Taylor stuck to his resolution. His traumatised family secretly watched him until he lurched out again. When he left they burst into speech, giggling nervously, eyes on the windows in case he returned. When his rattletrap spluttered to life, they felt great relief.

"Phew! I expected the worst!" Sidney laughed nervously.

"And so say all of us," his mother sang out.

"*Jisslaaik*! I thought for sure Da's gonna capsize the whole house, for real," Cohen grinned mock angrily. "If he did anything I was gonna do him!"

"Cohen! That's not funny at all!" Elizabeth was shocked yet inside she felt strongly that that would be a good day and she would personally bury his body and no one would ever know her son's dreadful secret. Taylor would just disappear. *"The Madden's would suspect but they won't ask, I'm sure, and they won't say anything. Only Cora must never even get a whiff of it."*

"Elizabeth de Vee!" she chided herself! "How can you pray to Almighty God when you have such a dirty heart? Shame on you!" *No one must ever know how she felt inside.*

"Respect!" she glared at each child in turn. "You are courteous, therefore you respect. Remember that. Your father is your father!"

"What a hypocrite I am," she thought.

"Yes, Ma," timidly and in unison. Neither she nor Cora saw the look and the wink that passed between the boys.

Taylor and Jordan met at the gate. Jordan was swearing loudly as he struggled to unlock the padlock. When he heard Taylor's van, he turned and waited for help. They behaved like school boys planning a day away from school.

"Ever heard of *The Cow Shed*, my friend?" asked Taylor.

"Vaguely," Jordan grimaced. "My head ain't working right. I should'a gone to you to get a lift. My van…"

"Yeah. Safe where it is. We'll start there."

"Cow shed, hey?"

"Cow shed, pal. That's where we'll put in some hard labour today, my friend." Taylor laughed. "I have a disease that needs only one cure."

"Yeah. And I need to start at an ATM. Leave your old boneshaker under the trees over there. We'll go in mine."

From the ATM they went to Perry's bottle store and then to their decided destination. The matron there was a nice lady, and very accommodating, for a fee. Manager and Foreman were having the day off.

"Today we be cow pats," Jordan said.

"Wha' dat?"

"Maybe it's good you dinno."

Taylor thought long and hard about that. Finally he roared with laughter.

"So, oh toothless one, your thoughts are killing you or is your personal spook tickling you?"

"Cow pat… cow shed… I gerrit."

No, you don't, bone head.

"Why we don' go to the pub when the men knock off an' join 'em? What say me ole pal, me ole matey?" Jordan asked, eyebrows raised, tone very English.

"Now you talking! An' you soun' like not-so-bonny Prince Charlie."

They cackled loudly and long, holding onto their tortured heads.

By the time they left the bar that night, they were too drunk to stand. One by one, the enormous, very strong Perry took them bodily over his shoulder and threw them quite unceremoniously into the back of Jordan's van. They would be safe there for the night. The cold of the early morning air would wake them and probably sober them up. He fetched late Fleabag's old blanket from under the bar counter and threw it over them.

Taylor woke up first. He sat up and looked around him.

"Hey, Jors, wake up." He shook his friend roughly. "Wake up! It's morning."

Jordan moaned pitifully, putting his hands to his throbbing head and swore roundly at Taylor. "My head… my head," he moaned. "Why did I do it? I'm ginne die." He closed his eyes and writhed in pain. Taylor looked at him empathising. "My head is cracking but I don' think I ginne die. I tell you this: nummer one… ou Teeza need a cure… nummer two, I ain't goin' near home now. They can won'er where I am till they lost!"

"Taylor, shut up! You making me worse." Jordan groaned pitifully. "Where are we?" Gingerly he sat up. "Outside Perry's!" he exclaimed. "Ow! My head! That … that … King Kong must've dumped us here." He laughed shrilly, tightly holding his throbbing head.

"We need some o' the dog's hair… some o' the dog's hair, ou maat."

"You think Perry keeps Fleabag's hair under the counter to cure this kind of sickness, ou pal?" Jordan looked as sick as he obviously felt.

That set Taylor snickering and then they were laughing painfully, holding onto their heads and then their stomachs. Hastily they crawled to the grassy patch close by and did what they had to do.

"No more o' that! I need a mouth wash," moaned Jordan, his red eyes streaming and his nose in stiff competition. Needs forced him to pull up a corner of his shirt to get relieved. He heard Taylor clear his sinuses behind him… one nostril at a time. *A-a-a-h*, he moaned silently and held his breath to keep from reacting.

"King Kong not ginne open till nine." Taylor turned around, wiping his hands across his backside. "Good name, good name. Juz right for him, ja, jus right for him, ja, ja, ja." He giggled carefully. "I need a fix right now. And I need a bottle o' pain pills." Taylor thought he had the solution to their problem. "Let's break into the pub. Perry will understand. He's a okay guy."

He seemed quite serious and Jordan began to laugh again, holding onto his pain-wracked head. "You serious, idiot? Did you forget Perry's house is behind the pub?"

"Hell, ou maat, I clean forgot. More better! Let's be gonners, then. No need for breaking an' en'tring. I nearly made us robbers," he chuckled.

"You talk too much, Taylor de Vee. You making me feel sicker. Let's go knock him up."

"Knock him up, hey? How you ginne do dat, ou Jors?"

"Shut up, you walking sewer pipe. I can't forgive myself. Two nights in a row! No!"

"We improving, ou maat. Show da liver who's da baas!"

"When I think of yesterday, I feel too bad. We did the wrong things, mate. Very, very wrong. What if Sylvie and Elizabeth find out?"

"Then you deny it, don'chu know? You never did nothing, ou maat. Also you let your fingers do da talking... Papa Fist!" He demonstrated, banging a fist into his other hand. "Mr Palm and his sidekicks."

"That easy, hey? Let's get going before my head explodes."

Very carefully they examined one another and began to laugh. "You look like a dog's breakfast," cackled Jordan, pointing at Taylor.

"You don't look so bad yourself," laughed Taylor. "Beautiful yesterday, beautiful today, beautiful forever," he chuckled holding onto his head more firmly.

"An' you don't smell half bad neither. Lavatory liqueur, for shore." He almost keeled over while the hammers in his head pounded away.

"Let's go look for Perry. One word out of him and its curtains for him," he threatened, making a cut throat motion as he said so.

"Perry will sit on you, skinny rat, and every bone in your body will shatter."

They crunched on the gravel making their way to the back of the pub. Perry was up. The door was open and the smell of coffee hung thick in the air. "That smell is bad for my stomach," whined Taylor.

When they got to the door, Jordan rattled the burglar gate and shouted for Perry.

"Well, well, well," Perry drawled. "If it isn't the troublesome twosome! Why was I actually expecting you, I wonder?"

50

He looked at them while he worked at the huge padlock. "Come in. I have just the right thing waiting for you, and it's on the house."

Taylor took a step back and looked up at the roof. "You got a ladder?"

"Don't be too clever, Taylor de Vee. You want a cure or what?"

"Very funny, but not funny enough," Jordan slapped him on the back. "But he's cute, hey Perry? On the house...on the house." He struggled to laugh with his head hurting more. "Of course we want that cure; we seriously ill."

When they were seated in the van again, Jordan turned to Taylor, "Where to, pal?"

"The township, ou maat… the township. They owe us a party!" The van roared and they were on the way.

Three days later they were still in the township.

The boys were convinced that their dads would be spoiling for a fight when they did return. They secretly made plans to forestall them.

"Drastic situations require drastic measures," one of them said and all agreed.

"This has nothing to do with respect and honour your parents," Cohen said.

"Too true, boo hoo. It has everything to do with bringing the monster within to justice." They had a humourous discussion that did nothing to mask the enormity of their decision.

"A guy's gotta do what a guy's gotta do," James said and they all sang, "And so say all of us."

"Every night we will go to the gate in disguise." Sidney said. "We have balaclavas and if you don't, we'll get for you three but you must give us the money to buy them. Necessary items!" Sidney was emphatic.

"Sure," James said. "I'll give you my savings card and I'm sure I can trust you with my pin. Then you can draw the bucks and get us the hoods. Soon! We need to be on guard by tomorrow night. They may even decide to come home tonight, who knows?"

They told no one in their families about their plan. Sidney, Cohen, James, Zane and Luke had what they thought was a fool proof plan. They'd wait, armed and balaclava'ed, in the bushes near the gate until their fathers returned from their 'holiday'. When the van stopped for Taylor to open and then close the gate, they'd strike. The plan was to hit hard and use their advantage of surprise before the men hit back and very possibly over-powered them. If they were lucky their fathers would be drunk and careless and clumsy.

As the hours passed, their thinking became more rational.

"Final reminder, guys, heads not to be cracked. We don't want to end up being father-killers. And we do *not* want them to be left spastic! They gotta work." James said.

"And if by any chance they're sober, we the ones who'll end up spastic," Luke cracked up. Their mirth was short-lived.

"Hey, Luke's right. If they sober we better act fast and do one thing. Pity we won't know…"

They waited.

They didn't have to wait too long. On their third night the vigilantes struck it lucky.

Suddenly…head lights!

"They saw us," hissed Sidney as they dived for cover.

"Shut up, Sidney, you just scared! How could they see us?" his brother hissed back.

The moment had come. The van was inside waiting for Taylor to lock up and get in again. Their angry sons rushed out. Without a sound their boys went to work on those cruel hands… and ribs…and legs…and arms.

As suddenly as they appeared, they vanished leaving two defeated, whimpering bruisers in the dust. According to plan they disappeared into the bushes again to race home by a very roundabout route.

When Jordan eventually crept into the house, he said not a word. Sylvia's relief was mixed with a sick feeling of what-next? Then she shrieked. He stared at her drunkenly. The children came running.

For once she was not abused by word or deed by her drunken husband. "Phew! I wonder when you last had a wash?" she thought. "You smell of the bottom of a badly neglected dirt bin."

"Dad!" the girls cried in unison.

"Ah…the return of the prodigal," Zane stated in obvious amusement.

"And in such bad shape. Tjo!" Luke tried his best to keep the laughter from erupting.

"Shame, Daddy, you remind me of Ma when you've done her up." James spoke very seriously.

The boys soon sent their sisters back to bed and ministered not too gently to their hurting, swollen, filthy father.

"You right, James, just look at that shiner! Ma, doesn't this look familiar?" Zane got a hard elbow in the ribs from James. "Leave Ma outa this," he hissed.

"What happened, Da'?" Luke asked.

"I dinno," slurred his father, his head slowly wobbling from side to side.

"Da's head is rotating on its own axis," teased Luke.

"Luke! Get out!" James's tone brooked no argument. Luke left but stood at the door to peep inside. "Tell us, Dad, what happened to you? You look like a train hit you." James persisted until his father slurred, "I think a troop of monkeys came at us." He soon toppled over while his boys were taking off his clothes and he fell into a deep drunken slumber.

"Not on the bed, he's too dirty," Sylvia said and they left him on the floor.

"I wonder what happened to your father, poor thing." She was genuinely concerned. It showed in her face and in her tone.

"Poor thing, my eye! He deserved every blow he got!" James looked fiercely at his mother. "How can you feel sorry for him when… when… Huh!" He was speechless!

The following day they did not see their father. Nor did they see him the next or the next. He remained in his room for as long as it took for his face to look reasonably normal again. By then he was threatened with dismissal from his job so he re-entered the world. He became quite docile after that. Kay was sure that the hiding had knocked sense into him.

"Best thing that could have happened to Dad," she declared.

"He needs to stay away from the bottle for the rest of his life. Too many bad memories too jammed up together," said Olivia.

"What a life! Poor Mom. He goes at her too, too much when he's been at the bottle. And it's almost every day now. I wonder who he fought with while he was away. I wish this hiding will keep him from drink for good!" Kay said feverishly.

"Yeah. And whenever he comes home drunk the monkeys should be waiting!" giggled Olivia. "Sonja went for him; did you hear what she said?"

"No, do tell," breathed Kay.

"She brazenly walked up to his bed and said, 'I'm glad you got hit; now you know how Ma feels when you hit her. I don't even feel sorry for you, Da' because it's a good lesson for you.' Then she turned on her heel, threw her head in the air as only Sonja can, and flounced out."

"Huh? Go, Sonja! That told him. She spoke for all of us."

"I think she's the only one with guts."

"You got that right, sis," grinned Kay. "Sonja deserves a medal."

"And who's the only one with guts?" James put in a sudden appearance. "Don't you believe it," he said and winked conspiratorially at Kay. He urgently put a finger to his lips and mouthed, "Later."

"Do I want to know?" she asked James when they met.

"Maybe you should remain in ignorance," James teased knowing full well she was burning with curiosity.

"Spill the beans, lug!" she pinched his arm hard.

"Ouch! That hurt," he exclaimed.

"There's more where that came from," she threatened.

"Ok, ok, violence is becoming a family thing! You pinch hard. Listen… you are closely related to the troop of monkeys…" and he dodged her fingers and ran off.

Kay stared after him with her mouth hanging wide open. "My brothers! The attacking monkeys! Well! I didn't think they had it in them. Done the old man a whale of a lot of good, too. He's become a pussy cat. Go, brothers! Good on you."

Back at the de Vee house, Taylor crawled in on his forearms and hurting knees. His fingers were badly injured.

Elizabeth screamed when she saw him and her boys came running, with Cora at their heels, wide-eyed with fear.

"Oh, it's you, Da'. Drunk… again… an' wounded. Shame. Gone five days an' you come home like this… Shame," she said and went back to her room.

"So said Cora!" Her mother was shocked.

"Yes, she's growing up." Cohen looked at his father. "Hey, Da', you don' look so good. You'n' yer pal have a rumble? What happened?" His boys moved to help him to his feet. Feigned or genuine, he collapsed, right there in the doorway.

"Pass out case," Sidney said. They could not hide their worry.

"He needs the hospital, Ma," Sidney said. "Looks bad, huh Cohen? Let's take him there."

"How? If Jordan and he were together, chances are he can't drive us there." Elizabeth was worried.

"Aunt Sylvie can drive…"

"He's stinking like the night cartage truck. Without a bath, he's going nowhere."

They dragged him to the bathroom and did the best they could.

Of course she had some explaining to do. "Ma, what's a night cartage truck?" Their disbelieving, "Gross!" had her in stitches.

Under the shower Taylor recovered enough for them to be convinced he did not need medical attention after all.

The encounter with "the monkeys" put the men on the wagon. "This time for good!" Jordan decided. He began to curse the day he tasted liquor. He began to hate the undeniable pull it had on him. He loathed the fact that nothing but another swig from the vodka bottle would satisfy him.

The urge was alive inside him. He went through each day, becoming increasingly morose, desperately fighting the monster inside that screamed for appeasement. He wanted a drink so bad it hurt. The battle between urge and logic was fierce. Peace with family meant this personal suffering. Flashes of a conversation with Taylor kept tugging at him. What had he said to the man? Now he had to take his own advice. How easy it is to advise when you don't know what it actually feels like. He cringed with shame.

"Maybe you have childhood issues you have to get out of your system…"

"When I see Elizabeth, my fists ball up…"

"Have you thought of seeing a psychiatrist?"

The boot was firmly on the other foot!

Kay and James turned sixteen in the same year and they decided on a combined party. Their dad and his boozing buddy were still on the wagon so James thought it would be fine to have a champagne toast. Kay fought it.

"I do not want us to have champagne. It is alcoholic! We all know what alcohol is doing in our home."

"Kay, lighten up. Dad's been sober for quite a while. He's not going to go back just because we have champagne at our party. And I don't see why we should deprive ourselves because of him!"

"Ok, James, but remember this – I do not need a champagne toast. I do not see myself as being deprived if we use apple juice instead! Water would do the job just as well. That's ok, laugh. What does toasting signify anyway? But have it your way. I'll stand down. Just don't say I didn't warn you."

What a party it was! They had a marquee out on the vast lawn. Their parents did not spare a cent! They were even more excited about it than the children were. Sylvia invited every family that had sent their children to "Sylvia's" right from its inception. She was so proud of her babies – sixteen.

Although Sylvia also did not want it, Jordan got champagne because he agreed with James that a champagne toast was the only way! They had a jolly good time and would have gone on until the morning if Taylor didn't decide to fall off the wagon that night. He did it with astonishing drama.

First he pulled Elizabeth up from her chair and shouted, "Let's jit, bokkie."

"Taylor!" she cried, "Don't pull me like that. I'm so-o-o tired. Let's sit this one out."

"You dirty cow …" and he proceeded to lay it into her. She screamed and that was enough for Jordan. He caught hold of Taylor by the scruff of his neck and threw him across the lawn.

Sidney and Cohen helped their father home and when they were indoors laid it into him. They kicked, they hit, they stomped all the while shrieking like banshees. Their pent up hatred was vented fully in those ten minutes. Then Cohen had to force Sidney to leave him. "Sidney, don't, we don't want to kill him."

"Speak for yourself, Cohen…" The overwrought Sidney turned away and went to splash cold water on his head. Then he left the house. Cohen bathed his father and put him to bed all the while rebuking him for the lousy human being he was.

"I told you so, Jordan Madden. I said no liquor. Now look at what's happened." Jordan dropped his head and gave Sylvia a sad, apologetic look.

When Sidney got back Sylvia and Elizabeth guessed immediately what had happened.

"Oh, Sidney! Son, what have you done?"

"Enough is enough, Ma. If he's started again then its shutters down for you. He'll kill you next time. Get packed; we're leaving."

"No, Son, not just like that. Where's Cohen?"

"He's putting Pa to bed."

"Your dad has been sober for so long! Tonight was just a mistake…"

"How do you know that, Ma? He's a hopeless, violent alcoholic!"

59

"Don't let your disappointment and anger make you jump to conclusions. The Madden's are putting us up for the night; we'll talk to daddy in the morning."

Then the other cow pat hit the fan!

The following afternoon Jordan staggered into the crèche. Sylvia was talking to a parent. She had called him to fetch his son who was running a high temperature.

Jordan saw a cosy set up in her little office and he blew up. The children began screaming and running wildly to get out the door. The parent tried to hold Jordan and that was the red rag! The bull charged! He fisted the man in the face. Blood splashed! Upper dentures flew…in two pieces! His head snapped back and he stumbled and fell backwards, sending kindergarten chairs and tables flying.

Pandemonium reigned! Sylvia screamed and the nannies sprang into action. From where he was in the house Luke heard the commotion and ran, convinced there was an invasion by robbers and criminals. He abandoned the assignment he'd skipped school to complete and ran.

"This is happening in my yard…in my home. What an eyeball!" And his stripe went up! His dad again! He grabbed him by the scruff of the neck and dragged him out, holding onto the door jamb and then the railing for dear life. Then they clattered down the steps and the howling, curious children scattered as they landed on the grass.

The injured parent was on his way to his motor car, hanky over his mouth with his son jog trotting alongside him. Sylvia gathered his broken dentures in a tissue and ran after him. She took the boy up in her arms and placed him in the back seat of their car. His dad would need medical attention as well.

Jordan lay on the grass looking up at Luke, venom in his eyes. "You little pipsqueak, I should have strangled you at birth." He was frothing at the mouth. "You saw your mother with that man…"

"If Mom was with a man I'd celebrate. She's suffered enough at your hand."

He struggled to get to his feet but his son's outstretched foot pushed him down every time.

"Let me get up," he screamed. "Get away from me."

The police showed up, guns at the ready. The offender was handcuffed and taken away. The upshot of the day's events was that 'Sylvia's' was shut down at once.

Around the dinner table the day's events were discussed.

James whistled soundlessly when the story was told. "Our father…what a man! Monster Man! Wonder Dad!"

"Your father will come right, don't give up on him," Sylvia pleaded.

"Methinks Pops has now out-Taylored Taylor."

After the man was recompensed in the small claims court the Madden's were left penniless. Jordan was also sentenced to a year in prison.

The year flew by and before they knew it, Jordan was released. Christmas loomed just ahead. The holidays! Everyone was home. Jordan behaved like a stranger, saying little, and keeping mostly to himself. His mind, however, was busy. There were plans to be laid and outcomes to be hatched. His one big bother: should he pull it alone, or could friend Taylor be trusted to help him?

Jordan had befriended some shady characters while he was incarcerated. He'd acquired a gun, ammunition enough for a small army and the habit of smoking dagga. He also joined the prison fitness club and worked out diligently each day. "I'm a Madman with a plan," he'd tell himself repeatedly. Because of his prowess in a fight, he had a following that kowtowed to him and jumped at his every whim in return for protection. Protection fees brought in all the money he needed for all he wanted. When he got out of there beware everyone who'd had a hand in putting him there! He'd begin with that Sylvia! The hatred he bore for her defied rationality.

Jordan got his job back. His friendship with Taylor took up where it left off. Taylor had a strange new respect for the man. No one had visited Jordan in jail because he refused to see anyone, "I have enough company here," he rudely told anyone who tried to see him.

Taylor continued to abuse himself and his family until he landed in hospital where he was treated and then discharged with the warning that he was on borrowed time…just a few more drinks and it would be curtains for him. He tried his best to remain sober. Irrationally he hated his liver and pancreas and thought their malfunction had nothing to do with him. He refused to relate his existence to two organs. Why shouldn't he drink just because of a liver he couldn't even see? He seemed to overlook the fact that drinking caused him terrible pain, but he had to admit: he had choices…drink or don't. That stupid doctor said drink and die. "It's your body, Taylor. You do what you feel is best for it. Its drink and die or abstain and recover. Right now your liver is in danger and cirrhosis is not reversible."

"That man think he's God!" he told himself, flinging out an arm dismissively.

He crept into his shell and became a nasty piece of work his family lived with, grateful that he was sober at least and there was no fight in him. He resented the thought that Elizabeth was well and healthy and he had a death sentence hanging over his head. Try as he might, he could not pin this on her. He thought of accusing her of poisoning him but realised that would not stick. Best thing was to keep his condition to himself. When he couldn't help doubling over in front of his family, he excused it with words of hate: "Your mother is trying to kill me. There must've been poison in my food."

No one dignified that with a reply.

Alone together Sidney said, "If Ma had brains she would poison him!"

"Hey! Dad is putting ideas into my head," Cohen sighed. "I wish he would change. So nice to have a father and mother but what's the use? This family is jinxed. And the Madden's are in the same boat now. Who'd have thought it?"

"Ja…I feel sorry for them. We used to it…they… but they gotta be used to it by now. Who knows – maybe their mother will leave…"

"Maybe not. Maybe she's also scared he'll kill her if she sets a foot out the door as Da' says to Ma."

"Me? I'm never ginne get married."

"Me neither, bro."

"Maybe we got his evil genes just waiting for the day to show up." They continued to joke about the things they'd be likely to do.

During Jordan's absence Taylor was like a man in mourning. He went nowhere except to work. He spoke to no one except at work. At home he pretended to read. He bought the paper each day and spent long hours with it or he watched sports shows …alone. The children visited the Madden's most of the time, and Elizabeth busied herself in the garden, with their fowls and doing whatever else would keep her from being in the same room with Taylor. "Avoidance tactics," she grimaced to herself.

Now the terrible twosome was back together again and officially on the wagon.

Taylor was won over and soon he was an eager dagga smoker, even polluting his bedroom with his longsuffering wife having to dumbly endure it.

"Hey, Sidney, can you smell what I smell?"

"Ja, phew, where's it coming from?"

"And so strong. Sidney, my lad, that is happening right here under our roof!"

"Da'… Da'? You think Da'…"

"I don't think, I know. That smell is the same wherever it is smoked."

With that they jumped out of bed and raced silently to their parents' door.

"One more word out of you, Elizabeth and you'll eat this joint. Shut up, you not goin' out that door."

"I need the toilet, Taylor," Elizabeth's pleading tone did nothing to soften Taylor.

"You goin' nowhere. Pee on the floor…pee on the bed. You got choices."

The boys raced back to their room.

"Tjo! Ma's in trouble. I can't believe Pa. I bet Jordan brought that habit from the chookie.

"Ja, monkey see, monkey do. I don't believe it!"

"Cohen, I'm worried 'bout Ma. Lemme think of something. What if I go in there and tell him what I think of this smell that's filling the house?"

"What if he jumps up and smashes your skull?"

"I know; I'll go in crying I'm sick an' I want Ma to help me."

They rushed out and the scheme worked. While Sidney was rushed to the bathroom by his mother, Cohen boldly walked in and addressed his father.

"Pa, if Pa has started smoking dagga, then Pa needs to go find another place to stay. This is all of our home and dagga smoking is against the law. It stinks and if we go to school smelling of the stuff how will we answer questions they will ask?"

Taylor put his stump out in the ashtray nearby and sat up straight. "Ah, my son faces me like a man. Ok, boy-o, fair enough. I just want to remind you who's the head of this house." He vigorously slapped his chest with both hands. "And I'll do what I want, when I want, where I want. And if you stick your nose in here to tell me nonsense in my bedroom again, I will cut it off. Move it up…now!"

Sidney and Elizabeth were back from the bathroom.

"Thanks, Ma, I do feel a little better. I think it's that bad smell that did it. What was it, does Ma know?"

"Ask Pa, he knows what was smelling," Cohen couldn't resist.

"Now, boys, go to bed. If you feel sick again, call me." She gave them both a kiss and sent them to bed.

One of the men was celebrating his fiftieth birthday and invited his workmates and their wives to a celebration in the local civic centre.

"Hey, ou Jors, if we go to that party we will be tempted again. I don't want that. Drink is killing me."

"Whatchu mean drink is killing you? You been off the pots, how long?"

"It's more'n that, ou maat. I have liver problems."

"Liver problems, hey…"

"…an pancreas problems."

"Yo! You got burial insurance?"

"Don' make a joke, ou maat."

"Joke? Who's gonna bury you if that thing kills you? Me? Not on your life, pal. An' your family will make you have a pauper's funeral." They found this funny and when their mirth died down, Jordan said, "You serious about the liver and pancreas? I s'pose we all gotta die. This world is one huge hospital an' we all on the last list. When your number's up, it's up, liver or no liver, pancreas or no pancreas. Ma-a-a-an, if the liver don' kill you, the taxi will."

"You are very comforting, ou maat."

"Facks is facks, mate. I may die before you… an' you won't take a cent outa your pocket. I got that all wrapped up. An' I got insurance… a lekker policy. If Syl kicks it, I'll be left sitting pretty."

"Hell, man, you did a wise thing. I'll see to it this week."

"I learnt some things in the chookie. I'll teach you more, but not all at once. The spliff an' the policy…enough for now. Jus' don' forget the policy. Don' say nothing about the liver an' the pancreas. That'll disqualify you. I know the doctor to see. He'll see you right." He took a deep breath. "I got plans, ou pal, serious plans. Go start that policy today… tomorrow… no later."

Jordan and Taylor went to the party without their wives.

Again the toasting of the honoured celebrant was their undoing.

Taylor nudged Jordan, "One can't kill us."

"Just a snort… sport," Jordan put on a fancy accent that had Taylor in stitches. "Tha's right, Prince Charlie," he chuckled. Jordan snatched a serviette from the table and stuffed it into Taylor's mouth. "Say it, don' spray it," Jordan hissed. This made the whole table crack up.

Of course, Jordan didn't need to be convinced. He'd abstained too long as it was. In prison he had none of the popular homebrew. He just did not trust it. When he got out he decided to lay low. Give his wife the impression he was a changed man. He'd show her who was boss.

Now Taylor made him think again. Why not? It was free, wasn't it? It's not as if they were in the pub where the liquor seemed to be laced with poison. That must be what made them so aggressive. Then he had a drink. He shot a neat vodka, shook his head with a deep groan and put down his glass. "Sis, but it's nice," he smiled at those close by who were attracted by his groan. He soon decided that one called for company. "That one din touch sides, my china," he said and beckoned to the waitron. Taylor was not to be left out.

And that was the start of yet another season.

Taylor's drinking binge was very short lived. His body rebelled violently.

Jordan made his family thoroughly miserable.

Again.

This time he could not resist using his latest acquisition, hitherto hidden. He had acquired a silencer and he smiled each time he thought up ways of tormenting Sylvia. He would not kill her as that would compromise his insurance policy claim. He was taking no chances. The police were not complete idiots.

His opportunity came when Sonja joined her siblings on a night out at the opera. An overseas company was presenting *The Barber of Seville*.

"I especially look forward to Figaro's aria," Sonya told her mother.

"What's an aria?" Sylvia wanted to know.

Sonya put on an imitation operatic voice to lah lah lah. "It's a solo in an opera." She laughed at the expression on her mother's face. "Obviously you no likee, Mama?"

Sylvia laughed out loud. "Country music concert? Oh, yes-s-s. Opera? No-o-o," she wailed in mock agony.

Leaving Sylvia alone was not a chance they wanted to take, but she convinced them that she would rather endure Jordan's mean temper than sit through the opera.

When Jordan got in from work she said nothing about Sonja's absence. However, he called her.

"Sonja," he shouted from his bed.

Sylvia's stomach sank. "She's with the others. They've gone to a concert."

"Oh. So they don't need my permission to go in to town at night, hey? What am I? A piece of rubbish?"

"No, Jordan, not at all. You weren't in or they must've forgotten or something. Anyway the children are not babies anymore. Just Sonja…and she's safe with her sisters and brothers."

Suddenly he sat up straight and rubbed his raspy hands with glee, grimacing at her. "So, we're alone together, after all these years. What a gift! What a blessing! Maybe angels are looking down at us and smiling."

Sylvia froze.

"What am I in for?" she asked herself, painfully wringing her trembling hands under the covers.

He threw back the covers on his side, jumped out of bed and stomped to his wardrobe. After rummaging for a few seconds, he straightened up. Smiling evilly at his wife, he held the gun up and nodded at her.

"You know what this is, Sylvie, me gal?"

"Of course, it's a… a gun." She was in shock. "What do you need a gun for, Jordan?"

"Don't ask rubbish. To wash my face? To braai my burgers? What do you think? To shoot, woman, and guess who I intend to

69

shoot?" While he spoke he got out the makings and prepared a spliff for himself which he lit up right there in the bedroom.

"Want a pull, dearest? Mary-Jane." He shoved the spliff up and down before her. "This is Mary-Jane. I want you two to meet. Go o-o-o-on, be a devil. Just one pull?" Mr Nice Guy coaxed. "It won't kill you…" Then his whole demeanour changed. "Bu-bu-but *this* will," and he held up the gun, threateningly and waved it slowly.

Unpleasant Mr Nice Guy.

Leaning back against the pillows, he smoked, leisurely and with obvious enjoyment. "This is so nice, Sylvie, me love. Just me 'n you… all on our ownsome. So-o-o-o romantic. You've no idea how many times I thought of a night like this ju-u-u-ust me 'n you…" The fear-gripped woman shook violently. Was this her last moment on earth? She closed her eyes and waited, trying her best to control her shaking. What was there she could say or do? "Oh, dear God, my children…"

"You praying? Shame; you poor, poor, unfortunate thing. Do they know you up there? Think they expecting you?" He laughed maliciously. "Don't worry – I'll make sure you have a great farewell. Open your eyes, Syllie, dearest, and sit up, there's a good girl." His sweet, kindly tone was extremely upsetting. He drew deeply on the foul cigar, blew the smoke at Sylvia and replaced it in the saucer on his bedside pedestal. He began to chuckle mirthlessly. "Syllie… silly. Geddit? You got a good name. You certainly are a silly woman."

He pushed a fist under her back and forced her up. She struggled up, staring at him in abject terror. Then he made a show of getting off the bed, kneeling as in prayer mode, his elbows on the bed.

"No, dearest, I'm not about to pray, though I should, for the soul of my soon-to-be-departed wife. The end is near, my precious Syl… for you!" he looked around the room as though seeking something.

"Ah," he exclaimed, "look there, my lovely, up there," he pointed at the framed pictures on the pelmet above the window. Then he took careful aim and shot to smithereens the picture taken of him and Kay seated on a low bench under the oak tree. Shards of glass flew in all directions, showering over the horrified woman on the bed and on him kneeling there. He swaggeringly blew the front of the gun, cowboy movie fashion, and winked at her. Her whole body recoiled. The bullet ricocheted and landed against the wall behind Jordan. It rolled across the floor and he watched it come to a stop.

"The next is for you, lovey-duck."

She cowered and drew the blankets over her head, jabbering wildly. He lifted the gun and slammed it into her shoulder.

"Uh-uh, that's not how it's done. You sit up straight and watch Papa Bear."

"Jordan… Jordan, please. Do what you're doing. I don't have to watch you kill me."

"I've changed me mind, dearest. See that picture there… on tha-a-a-t wall? It's our only wedding picture. Remember that stupid day? It will have its turn now." Again her whole body recoiled at the sound. Her throbbing shoulder needed attention but she daren't take her eyes off this mad man. Then he caressed the silencer, smiled at her and said, "Your turn's coming. Don't be impatient. Hang in there."

He looked slowly around the room, seeking his next target.

"A-a-a-h, oh silly one, my next target. See there… see there, Sylvia. Leave that shoulder! You won't feel it at all, just now. In fact you won't feel anything." His laugh was eerily like a sinister Hitchcock character. "Look… over the-e-e-re." He drew the word out high pitched. She looked at the beautiful lampshade in the corner of the room where his one-time reading chair had stood. Made of porcelain, they had bought it at an auction sale when they had first come out to the farm. It used to be a proud possession.

"Oh, Jordan, please I beg of you, not that lamp. It used to belong to…"

"…then you can report me when you join them a little later," and he shot it. A huge spray of gravelly porcelain scattered around the room and the smell of paraffin permeated the place.

The frenzied woman screamed. He turned on her, "Your turn!" and then, "BANG!" he shrieked maniacally and cracked out laughing crazily. He threw the gun on the bed and himself alongside it and laughed uncontrollably.

Sylvia looked at the gun and at him and with a superhuman effort overcame the temptation. Silently she slid under the covers and pulled the blankets over her head. The joint Jordan had been smoking fell from the ashtray onto the floor and the smell of burning soon invaded the room. They reacted simultaneously. She got up and raced to investigate. He straightened up and looked at her.

"A-a-a-h, my wife, my life, my bride. Where to?"

"Can't you smell? Something's burning."

"Ok. Do your thing."

Fortunately the paraffin from the shattered lamp had not spread that far. She knelt down to scrape the smouldering cigar into the ashtray and he assaulted her from behind. What saved her was the sound of Taylor's old jalopy arriving. The noisy vehicle caught Jordan off guard for some reason and he left the room to peep through the dining room window. Sylvia grabbed the opportunity. She snatched up her gown and slippers, pussyfooted to the unlocked kitchen door and went to sit on the front doorstep until the children got back.

She heard him stumbling around, shouting her name, threatening every vile act of indecency before and after killing her.

The awakening birds in the eaves above aroused her. Memories rushed at her. The children! They were still not back! She was aghast. If anything had happened to them, she was a dead woman for sure.

Then she heard James's car come in at the gate. She was so relieved that her bladder betrayed her right there.

Getting to her feet, she went to meet the car. They tumbled out boisterously, doing their best opera imitations.

"Better early in the morning than late at night, hey, Mums?" James teased her. "And why is my Mums waiting for us outside in this cold, cold morning air?"

"Oh, Mama, have you spent the night here? You're ice cold!" Kay drew her shivering mother closer. Her effort to keep calm failed and Kay held her while she cried bitterly. Olivia and Sonja joined the group hug.

Sylvia told the children a very watered down story. Eventually they trouped inside. All agreed to know nothing when they faced their father. All determined to perform like award winners. Sylvia would pretend she had been hiding inside all the time. They were relieved to hear his snores from the back door.

73

After greedily slurping warming mugs of creamy cocoa, they trooped to bed. Silently Sylvia cleaned up the room while her husband roared away on the broad of his back. "Thanks be… the children didn't see this unholy mess," she told herself.

That was the turning point in Sylvia's life. She determined in her heart that the end had come. It looked like a kill-or-be-killed situation and she had no intentions of having anyone's blood on her hands. And, horror of horrors, her children must not soil their hands!

She seriously contemplated asking Jordan the important Big-D question.

Before that day came she had to endure yet another gruelling experience.

Jordan thought up something so evil, even he felt he'd outdone himself. The de Vee's were celebrating Sidney's birthday. He'd do his deed on that night when their house was empty. Oh, yes! That was the perfect opportunity. There'd be loud music and a large noisy crowd of youngsters in the de Vees back yard. He grinned with glee and rubbed his hands in joyful anticipation.

The Madden's left together to attend the eagerly awaited braai and swaai (barbecue and dance). The Madden house was separated from the braai spot by the old oak and the de Vee house. There was huge open ground in that area en route to the dam. Taylor and his boys had pitched a large boma-style tent there, with a roof and open sides.

The party was in full swing. Friends had been invited, the tent was packed with a rollicking, jolly, mixed crowd and they sang and played music and danced to their hearts' content. They even had

74

karaoke. The chosen song was played softly and the singer would use a mike to superimpose their voice over it.

Taylor and Jordan periodically disappeared for a while and the smell that permeated the atmosphere announced their deeds. They came back arms around each other, singing lewd songs Jordan had learnt in prison. Their families pretended not to notice. Everyone was too embarrassed to acknowledge what they were hearing from these father figures.

Jordan became restless. There was something he had to do. If he didn't act now, when would be the right time? He'd time it perfectly... in that very short space between songs.

"Now!" he told himself. Suddenly he doubled up and groaned loudly. All attention was turned to him. He moaned pitifully indicating his stomach was hurting badly.

"Maybe it's his appendix," someone shouted.

"Emergency!"

"Take him to the hospital." All kinds of advice was shouted out.

Then Jordan slowly straightened up. "No, manne, it's ok... I'm ok. 'Twas just a passing spasm... a nasty cramp. Maybe I ate that chop too fast. I'll be ok. Jus' need to stretch out on my bed a bit. These cramps sometimes happen. Sylvie, come with me, ou girl, an gimme some o that bitter medicine... essence o' life."

Sylvia's heart sank. She sensed this was a ruse. She pinched Kay hard on the thigh as she laboriously got to her feet. None of her children rested easy as they watched them go, Jordan leaning heavily on her, keeping up the pretence. As soon as they were out of sight, Jordan turned on her. He was confident that the music was shield enough for any sounds that may spoil his fun.

The twittering in the oak tree had died down – the resident birds were asleep. She slipped and tripped on a slippery root encrusted with bird droppings and he yanked her up unceremoniously. He dragged her indoors and tied her hands behind her back. All resistance was slapped out with one hefty backhand. Then he forced a wad of tissues into her mouth and gagged her. Next he took her through the front door and out to the front lawn.

"We're going for a ride, sweetie pie," he laughed merrily. It was dark and the illuminated skyline from the party spot brought the outline of the houses and trees between them into sharp relief. It also served to heighten the darkness that surrounded them.

Her horror was made complete when he tied her to the back of his van with a longish rope. She could actually hear his maniacal laughter as he drove the car, pulling her along at a speed she could barely keep up with. She was gagging and weeping making hoarse sounds that hurt her throat. Then her world began to swim and she was out and down with a sickening thud. He dragged her inert body a few metres then stopped.

"Mustn't kill her," Jordan scolded himself, "Just shock her a bit. She's gonna make us rich! Reech! Lotto go to potto! I got me my own plan… beeg time! The po-li-cee, hee hee hee-e-e-ee!" His brain was pickled. Dagga and alcohol made an explosive mix in his system.

Then suddenly in the headlights … his children.

He restarted the engine… murder in his eyes. They scattered when they saw his intention. He drove off at a very high rev and almost immediately slammed the brakes.

"My policy!" He suddenly remembered.

The whiplash effect flung Sylvia bodily into the rear of his car. The screaming children hastened to their mother.

The party music stopped momentarily. His children's screams filled that crucial moment. The partygoers were electrified. Then they were galvanised into action. They ran to find out what was happening.

The authorities were called and the unconscious woman was taken to hospital, where she was put into ICU. Jordan was taken off to jail to await further proceedings and the angry, mournful children went home to comfort each other.

"Why didn't I act on my suspicions and follow earlier?"

"No-o-o-o. NO! Dad's lost it completely."

"I hate him with all my heart."

"I wish he would die! Tonight! Wish the police kill him in that cell. Who's that prisoner who was pushed out of a top floor window?"

"I know who you talking about. But that's politics. This is a domestic situation... attempted murder!"

"Ou' father, hey? Who'd have thought he'd become such a...a..."

"... Monster! He's the monster's bogeyman if you ask me!" Uneasy giggles.

"Alfred Hitchcock would've learnt quite a bit from him!"

"Apart from the de Vees, are there other families that suffer under their father's madness?"

"Hey! That's a question."

"I read somewhere that family violence is widespread. Didn't dream at the time it'd reach our happy home. Can you believe it? I actually turned that page and thought 'not in our home'."

"Wow! Look at us now."

"I always felt so sorry for the de Vees. I wished Aunt Elizabeth would poison him or put him out or something."

"Ma should do that. Da' is just not a person."

"What's a bogey man's monster, Kay?"

"Oh, Sonya, baby," Kay said and they all giggled. "A monster's bogey man. When the monster mama frightens her children, she says 'I'll call Jordan Madden to fix you up!' He's their bogey man."

"That's nasty. Daddy is nasty." She began to sob pitifully. Soon the girls were in tears, too. The boys went to their room.

James went off to the kitchen. "Cocoa all?"

A combined please followed him.

The boys returned to the girls' room. "Safe to come in? Waterworks turned off?"

They drank slowly sipping and blowing carefully.

Then James spoke into the silence.

"This is our father. Treating our mother like this!"

"They must have been in love at some time…"

"…if this is what love grows into, thanks, but no thanks!"

"Modern day horror movie producers also need to visit Dad… with their note books!"

"Yep! We're living our own real life thriller-cum-horror story. And it's not thrilling at all!"

Kay ended the meeting with, "The question is: where to from here? When Mama comes out of hospital, we can't continue under Dad's roof, and he's not going to stay here alone!"

James, too, was adamant. "Dad needs to be institutionalised. He must go, not us! He's cracked! Over the overs!"

They washed their cocoa mugs and turned in.

Jordan was released on bail the following day and returned to his house rebellious and defiant. His whole demeanour reinforced what he said, "Let's roll! One word out of you and it's…" finger-across-the-throat.

"That's my Daddy," Sonja sang out. He ignored her.

Sylvia made a slow recovery. Kay and Olivia gave up school. "Indefinitely, Mama. There's nothing you can say that will change our minds."

There was no case against Jordan. The papers mysteriously disappeared. Sylvia decided to drop the case because it was all so humiliating to have to repeat the story so many times to so many different Officers who treated her with disdain, questioning the truth of her statement. The papers simply disappeared without a trace. Jordan tormented her about that. "It's not WHAT you know, Syllie, me gal; it's WHO you know…"

He'd remind her constantly of her joyride "not quite in the back seat" and he'd bray loudly, head thrown back. "Wanna go for another ride, Syllie, me gal?" Bedtime was torture and her offer to go and sleep with the girls so he could sleep more comfortably, met with a dangerous, "Just you try, dearest… just you try. Your place is right

here next to your hubby. For better or for worse, hey? Just wait 'n'
see, me dear – the worst is yet to come."

Sylvia had finally reached the end of her tether. She was biding
her time. Suddenly something rose up within her late one Friday,
when Jordan staggered in from work. The time had come. She set his
dinner before him and calmly told him that she was leaving him and,
furthermore, she wanted a divorce!

Kay and Olivia were unashamedly eavesdropping. Sylvia's words
stunned them just as much as they must have stunned Jordan. There
was a deadly silence before Jordan began to laugh. It was an ugly
sound that made one's back and scalp feel invaded by a million
creepy crawlies. Kay had her mouth wide open and a hand firmly
over it. Olivia was beaming: "Go, Mama," she whispered, doing a
dance with her hands and hips. Then Jordan's chair scraped back and
the roar he gave was not human!

"DIVORCE, HEY!? I'LL GIVE YOU A DIVORCE!"

Sonja, rudely awakened, came running along. The girls burst into
the dining room which adjoined their parents' bedroom just as their
door slammed shut. Sylvia tried her best to muffle her screams of
pain. Sonja ran to the door and pounded on it with clenched fists.
"Open this door, you monster!" she cried over and over. "Open it
right now."

"Daddy, please don't kill my Mama," Sonja wailed loudly.

"Those words from Sonja made the gall rise up in me," Olivia
said later. "I actually tasted the bitterness, I swear!" Hatred of the

worst kind exploded within her and she lost control. Kay tried to stop her but backtracked fast when Olivia turned on her. She picked up a chair and with all her might, powered by hate and anger, smashed the door in.

"He'll kill you and Mama for this!" Kay hissed.

"Don't frighten me," Olivia sneered and then Kay's stripe shot up. "Count me in," she whispered hoarsely, shoving Olivia aside.

Kay stomped into the room, took a swipe at her dad who lost his balance and keeled over onto the trunk against the headboard and down onto the floor. Sylvia was on her knees. Sonja jumped to her side and she lifted her face to look at her children. Her face was a mess! Her injuries had injuries! What was left of what she'd been wearing hung from her in tatters.

Then Olivia really saw red! As she later said, "I swear I got the smell of blood in my nostrils! I flew at Dad and we had an old-fashioned knockdown-drag out right there in his bedroom. Truth to tell he defended himself without hitting me. I went for him! I was the tigress and Mama was my cub! I scratched. I bit. I screamed. I swore. I grabbed him by the hair and twisted with all my might. Finally I was spent and collapsed on the floor, shaking violently." Then she giggled. "And for my pains, I banged my shin on a corner of that old trunk! Double ouch! It's my daddy dent."

Sylvia's body was black, purple and blue. She ached all over. Her body was so sore she winced with every move she made. She was convinced her internal organs were ready to explode or something! She had pains inside in places she was not previously aware existed!

Jordan left.

Much to everyone's horror, Jordan was back the following night.

Temporarily as it turned out.

He stumbled into his bedroom. Flinging himself onto the bed, he went into a snoring deep sleep that lasted a short while. Sylvia managed to pull herself from under him and make a bed on the floor alongside.

Suddenly…

"*Sylvia! You dirty piece of rubbish, you! Where are you?*"

"I'm here, Jordan. I'm on the floor right next to you, dear," she managed to squeak placatingly as he threshed about on the bed, wildly seeking her.

Sylvia shook like a leaf in an autumn wind. She gritted her teeth to still their rattling. Tightly clenched fists pressed up against her mouth bruising her quivering lips. Knees were pressed hard against her twisting, writhing insides. "Please let this nightmare stop," she prayed fervently.

Her body ached from the previous night's assault. She was red and black and blue over most of her body. Her eyes were like those of a koala bear. It amazed her that she could actually see out of the little slits in the badly discoloured mushy flesh. She groaned with every move she made.

"Dad's at it again. Olivia… Olivia wake up." Kay shook her sister.

"Hm? Oh, Dad! I wish he'd fall under a moving truck!" Olivia rubbed her eyes. "After last night you'd think he's worked out his viciousness."

The boys came rushing into the girls' bedroom.

"I wish the man would drop dead," James said passionately.

"Why don't we do something about it... NOW!" Luke rubbed his hands, a determined glitter in his eyes.

"I can't take this," Zane said, his eyes teary with anger. "This is just too much. Last night was evil... HE is evil... and I call him DAD!"

The threshing stopped and the howling one reached out and switched on the bedside light. He looked daggers at his wide-eyed, fear-stricken wife. "Put your foot out that door, Sylvia, and it's you and I!" he hissed. "I'll chop off that scrawny neck of yours and bury you in the backyard. Just try to leave. Just you try." His voice dripped pure venom and he sprayed his foul liquor-tainted spittle all over her. She dared not wipe it away.

She stared at him – petrified, blinking rapidly as his spit hit her eyes, not daring to protect her face or to wipe the stuff away lest it antagonise him further. Pathetic little moans escaped from deep in her throat. She tried so hard not to cry out loud. The children must not be disturbed again.

"Listen there... he's forgotten...or he thinks its last night. He's continuing last night's reign of terror."

"Dad's losing it... big time."

"He's lost it, long time already. Why don't we just rush him and carry him out before it gets too bad."

Giggles...

"That sounds like a good idea, but who will bell the cat, huh? Let's wait a bit. Maybe he won't lift his fists,"

"And maybe the moon will change places with the sun."

"The man terrifies me. Worse, he's Dad. Can we lay hands on our father?"

"Why not? He lays hands on our Ma."

"I gave him what-for last night."

"And me. I should've smashed his ashtray over his head."

"I wonder why she stays. This is being a pig for punishment."

"Women have killed for much less."

"Seems this is a situation where a killing will end it all."

"Please, God, don't let that happen."

"Amazing… Sonja still asleep in spite of the racket."

He was back in the situation as though the hours between hadn't happened! The memory flitted across her mind. She'd suggested a divorce for she was certain he had no use for her. She remembered his reaction. She moaned pitifully… not again…he'd kill her. "My children," she whimpered soundlessly.

Silence.

Was he asleep? She dared not look up to see.

Suddenly he began to grind his teeth and to cluck his tongue. Startled she looked up, a shudder of revulsion rushing right through her. His eyes glittered insanely. She cringed at the horrible sight and sound.

Hypnotised, she stared into those crazy eyes. To her bewilderment his eyes softened. A sickening smile spread across his drunken doughy features. Then he spoke, friendly like. "In fact, Sylvia, my dearly beloved, I've changed my mind… you wanna go… go!"

The monster reared its head and roared, eyes bulging, neck veins rope-like.

"Go now! Get outta this house… NOW. NOW." He burst into a nasty sputtering cough and then continued, wiping his mouth with the back of his hand. The disturbing cough continued… "You have my blessing. You have my full, unconditional permission to get the heck outta here. You know, I have longed for this opportunity to get rid of you." He threw back his head and laughed maniacally.

"Listen to that. Is Dad right upstairs?"

"I can't believe what I'm hearing."

"That cough! Crikey! Sounds like he has serious lung problems."

"Die, you dog!"

"I wonder what Ma's doing. She must be in serious pain."

"She refused to see a doctor."

When the spluttering cough-laughing stopped he sat up on her side of the bed with his stinking feet on her chest. "Here," he forced her hands from her mouth with a heel. "Have you ever tasted your man's toes? Other women kiss their men's toes. You never did." While he spoke he wriggled his toes into her mouth, holding her down with the other foot. His arms behind him wedged him up.

"Gross!"

"Eek… that can't be for real."

"I want to vomit. Yuck! Have you smelt Dad's feet?"

"That is so-o-o-o sick!!"

"I don't believe this."

"Ma should bite his toes right off."

"Just listen to that!"

Nervous, embarrassed giggling.

"Nice, hey? Lekker, lekker?" he giggled and then let out a blood-chilling yell as her teeth clamped down hard on his toes.
"I knew it! She bit him!"
"Go Mama!"
"Yo! What's he gonna do now?"
More nervous giggling.

With her finger nails she clawed at his ankles using them as a pulley to drag herself up. She got as far as standing upright. He caught hold of her and yanked her down again.
"You bite me! Dog! You bite *me*? The one that puts food on your table? Ungrateful sod! Father of your children! Serpent! Where's your respect? I should do one thing with you now!" He kicked and stamped on her mercilessly, screaming vile words all the time.
Wretched sounds of fear and anger resounded from the fear-gripped children as they clung to each other yelling and swearing.
Then he stretched back and took the water jug that stayed on his bedside pedestal. Growling loudly, like a tortured animal, he dumped the water on her and continued his tirade. "And you leave with the wet clothes on your back, woman! Well, what the blazes! I bought those! I bought that nightie. I remember the day! It cost me a bundle, too. You go out as you came into this world!"
"What's he planning now?"
"Maybe we should rush in and rescue Mama."
"And what if that makes him madder? He never hits us. He'll take it out on her."

86

"I feel really sick. That's my mother…"

"Hold it. Wait. We all feel lousy. We'll see what happens. If it sounds like he's hitting her, we'll rush him."

While he screamed, and quick as her aching body allowed, she scrambled clumsily to her feet. He reached out and grabbed hold of her by the wet nightie. She strained bravely to get away from his tight grip and in the process he sprawled onto her makeshift bed on the floor. The high-pitched screech of the ripping nightie filled the place. With a super effort he gripped her by the foot and pulled her down onto him. He managed to turn over and get hold of her in a fierce grip.

The panic-stricken listeners, now tense and silent, were visibly shaking. Then James jumped to his feet but Kay yanked him back. "Wait," she hissed. "When we go, we all go."

Jordan worked his way upright and jerked his terrified wife to her feet. Slamming her onto the bed, she sprawled with her knees on the floor and her chest on the bed. He took hold of a handful of her hair and held on tightly.

With a violent jerk he pulled her up, viciously stripped her bare, digging into her flesh with his jagged, grease encrusted finger nails, and dragged her to the door, knocking her shins painfully against the rusted corner of the antique trunk that stayed against the bottom headboard.

At this point the listening children were beyond terrified. Tears flowed and teeth rattled.

Sonja, the youngest, chose that moment to wake up.

"Wh…what's happening?" She sat up and rubbed her eyes, looking around her, dazed. Her siblings, she noticed, were absolutely terrified.

"It's Dad again. He's back and he's on the war path as usual."

"I'm going out to tell him off!"

She slipped out of bed.

Her horrified sisters cried out. "No, Sonja, what if he gets stuck into you?"

"The other night I wasn't scared. What's wrong with me now?" Olivia quavered.

"Don't cry, Olivia," Kay put her arms around her. "I have a feeling this is Dad's last gasp effort. Things can't get worse. Sonja, wait… don't… he's not right in his head."

"Come back, baby, he's gonna hurt you." Olivia tried bravely to hold back her tears.

Her brothers made no attempt to stop her.

"Let him try!" Sonja, shoulders set, stalked off with head held high, dogged determination blazing from every pore. With her tousled curls hanging about her shoulders, and her long frilly nightie, she was a picture book character in a fairy tale. Off she flounced to get there just as her father was dragging her naked mother down the passage towards the kitchen.

"Daddy!" Sonja screamed. "Dad! Where are you taking Mama! She's got nothing on! Mama's got no clothes on!" She squeezed passed him, raced into the kitchen and grabbed a poker that was lying near the wood-and-coal stove. Brandishing it in the air, she screamed shrilly, "Daddy!" Then her voice dropped to a spine-chilling tone, and her words, like hailstones against a window pane, came staccato-like. "Leave. My. Mama. At. Once." Her voice rose to a scream. "Leave my Mama at once or I'll jab this in your stomach!"

She looked so fearsome that Jordan let go of his burden and faced his irate last-born, the apple of his monstrous heart. In that moment the devil that lived in him manifested in his little girl. She was prepared to kill him.

He saw it in her eyes.

The boys heard *no clothes* and it drove them.

"Kay! Olivia! Go help Sonja. If he lifts his hand to you, I'll come and help you." That was James.

"Why don't you go help Mama?"

"Didn't you hear Sonja say she's naked? I can't," he wailed mournfully.

When Kay came on the scene with Olivia close on her heels carrying her gown to cover her mother's nakedness, Sonja looked like a miniature warrior preparing to skewer the enemy.

"Sonja!" Kay screamed, "Put it down! Put it down, love; please, there's a good girl." Wild eyes turned slowly to her big sister. Then she flung the poker down and flew into Kay's arms. Olivia covered her mother and she called for James. He came and forcefully snatched his father by the arm. He pulled the unresisting man, caught off-guard, to the kitchen where he gave him a drink of water.

"What I need is vodka... cane, even better... not water! That mother of yours drives me round the twist!"

"What has Mama done, Dad?"

"She wants to leave me…us. Who does she think will look after us when she's gone? Hey? Hey? You tell me that. Maybe she has another man. She's got something up her sleeve!"

"Maybe she's just very, very tired of being treated like a punching bag by you!?" James tried his best to sound respectful. Mustn't antagonise the man further… this fire needed to be put out, not stoked.

"What did you say, boy? Punching bag? Punching bag? Did she tell you I treat her like a punching bag? That dirty cow is putting my children against me! When did I ever treat her like a punching bag? Of course I slap her around a little now and then when she's silly. She's my wife…I can do anything to her. And don't be fooled by all those marks…she has ways of making herself look as if I was panel-beating her."

"Dad, none of us will ever forget the night you tied Mama to …"

"…ok, ok, so I went overboard…you see how mad she makes me? What sane man'd do that to his wife, hey? Hey? Tell me that!" he screamed right into James's face. "She makes me so-o-o-o mad! She makes me flippin' flappin' stark staring mad!" James tried his best to keep the foul moisture from his face.

Luke snickered in the background. "Ole man's spraying you, James, here," he pushed a hanky at him.

James nodded his thanks at his brother then pulled up two of the individual-seater benches that stayed under the kitchen table and they sat facing each other.

"We're not fools, Dad," James continued, wiping his face in an exaggerated manner. "We may be your children but we're not children anymore and our ears and brains work as well as anyone else's. We hear you bash our Mama around almost every night… every night! We don't like it at all."

"You don't like it a' *tall*, hey? You don't like it a' *tall*." He threw back his head and laughed. It was maniacal and mirthless. "Hear that Sylvie? He doesn't like it a' *tall* when I bash you around." His swaggering body language mocked Sylvia's humiliation. The bench swayed dangerously. James stretched out a staying hand which proved unnecessary. He steadied himself and lurched to his feet. James followed him out.

Sylvia was trying to drink the water that Olivia had brought her. Her teeth rattled against the rim. Kay was nursing her mother's bruises and helping her hold an ice pack to her eyes. Sonja knelt on the floor with her head on her Mama's lap.

"Tell them, Sylvie, have I ever beaten you just for the hell of it?" he roared, rushing closer to her, head thrust forward.

James quickly stepped between them. Luke stood at the ready with Zane at his side, set for action. Their faces registered their feelings. The girls drew closer to their mother.

"You like a little bashing around don't you? Exciting, hey? Puts a bit o' spice in the works, hey, Sylvie? Gwaan, Sylvie, tell 'em. Remember the joy ride you asked for to feel what it was like when it happened at the bioscope…hey? You wanted to feel how it feels, didn'tchu? Tell 'em… James thinks I was trying to hurt you. Tell "em also what a hard-headed woman you are." He was ranting wildly, foaming at the mouth, eyes wild. "You are the most rebellious, most disobedient, worst-mannered woman in this country! Why I married you I'll never know! *Never*! If murder wasn't a crime, I'd've killed you long ago! Lo-o-ong ago! You hear me?" He straightened up and looked at all present. Then he lowered himself and rasped, "Open your mouth and speak…tell my children what kind of mother they have!"

"Here, wipe your mouth," James forced the hanky into his hand. He gave James what Zane called the evil eye, rudely snatched the hanky, and used it at once.

Sonja sat up. She spoke in a deadpan voice, with all the venom a child of twelve could muster, pronouncing each word clearly and separately. "Shut up, Dad. I wish you were dead! I wish you'd fall down dead right now, right in front of me. You are a mean, horrid, drunken, nasty…" she ran out of words and burst into tears.

James pulled his seriously wobbling father onto a chair he dragged against the wall.

"There, there, love; we all feel that way." Kay walked round her mother's chair to comfort her sister, her eyes fixed on her father. "It's a sin to hate your father and want to see him dead, but I think we've all had enough." Her loathing overwhelmed any fear that remained. "You are a non-human, and all your children hate you. Mama has not put us against you as you like to say. You did that all by yourself! You think we like to hear you swear at Mama like you do? That night was a scene from a horror movie and you say Mama asked for it!? With a wad of tissues in her mouth and a gag around her face? And your policeman friends think you did a good thing! Huh! You deserve to be hanged! Just how do you think we feel? Hey?"

Hysteria after prolonged pent-up fury. She, too frothed and foamed as she raved at her father. Zane grabbed an apron from the girls' room and thrust it at her. She grabbed it and threw it angrily on the table. When the tirade ended she reached for it, looked at Zane with a small smile of thanks and used it. Zane shuffled embarrassedly.

James cleared his throat with clear intentions.

Silence.

He spoke to Jordan, arms akimbo.

"Dad, I humbly ask you to leave the house and go stay somewhere else. We are your children and we did not ask to come into this world. You made us and now you are driving us insane with your behaviour. Liquor seems to have pickled your brain and it sees bad as being good. Mama's not your child. You speak as if you have every right to punish her when you think she did something wrong. If you abused your children in this way you'd be jailed..."

"And the key to your cell destroyed," shouted Zane.

James gave him a malignant look and continued: "We live here too and the only wrong doer we see and hear is you. You, Dad. There is nothing Mom does that I can see is wrong except put up with you and not pour boiling oil over your head when you're asleep. I say that in all sincerity. I have struggled to respect you regardless, telling myself the problem's with you and your wife and not with your children. My reasoning was probably based on fear. No more fear, Da'. No. More. Fear. I've crossed that line. I've hated you for a long time. I absolutely loathe you!"

Jordan listened, his bleary, red eyes fixed on his eldest son.

James hadn't finished.

"Please leave, Da', I beg of you, on behalf of us all. Take your clothes and go! Pack all your stuff into the back of your van and get out! We will all be glad to see the back of you. And you know what,

Dad? I cannot believe I am speaking to my dad like this…and it's liberating."

Jordan lumbered to his feet with all the drunken dignity he could muster.

"Luke!" he roared. "Go ask Taylor for his whip. This young puppy here needs a thorough whipping!"

"Dad, if I bring that whip, I'll use it on you!" Luke's voice was dangerously low. "We are right behind James in what he says. You need to thank James for being alive still… I have wanted to do one thing with you for a long time! I even began to hate my own mother for staying here and putting up with this…this…this nonsense of yours!"

"And I am not quiet because I have nothing to say, Dad," Zane spoke up. "Take careful note of what Luke has said…it goes for me, too. I think the girls have also had enough although I don't think they had murderous thoughts."

"Don't be too sure about that," Olivia burst out. "Don't you be too sure about *that*!"

Jordan turned around, holding onto the wall and walked into his room close by. He laboriously sought out his van keys and lurched out, almost tripping down the shallow step that led into the kitchen. Luckily, he grabbed the door jamb and steadied himself. He ignored the snickers behind him. Sylvia cast an angry eye at them.

"I'll be back tomorrow to fetch my things. Get them packed!" he snapped at Sylvia before slamming the outside kitchen door behind him. He was still in his pyjamas.

James ran after him. "Don't bother, Dad; I'll have your clothes waiting for you, at the turnstile gate. If you're late, the plastic bags and cardboard boxes will be there. Alone. Hopefully no one will steal them."

Jordan gave his son the one finger salute without looking at him and got into his van.

An image of his daughter stayed with him. He didn't need to close his eyes to see her standing there, brandishing that poker in the air. A comical sight, but it did not make him laugh. Then another memory visited his busy mind. Her cries were heart rending. "Daddy, please don't kill my mama." Did she realise what a thorn in his side her mother was? They'd be better off without her! It was all her fault… the dratted wretch! She was destroying his children… influencing them to do and say things that were just not right! Deliberately putting them against him. Hey! He had a disquieting thought. "Maybe the dirty b**** has a policy and is stirring up the children to do me in?" He laughed gutturally, his head thrown back. "She dinno me-ee. I'll do my thing before she can get her little nose in."

Between Kay and Olivia Sylvia was cleaned up, wincing and groaning pitifully.

"I bitterly regret not crashing the dressing table stool over Dad's head," Kay exploded.

"My girls," Sylvia's feeble voice made her girls want to weep. She beckoned them closer. "My girls, please don't tell your brothers about this. I am so afraid they will kill him or something one day. Thank you, Olivia, for defending me like you did, but it is not right to lift your hand to a parent."

"Dad provoked us, Mama," Sonja piped up. She burst out crying and wailed loudly, "I pray for him to change every night but things get worse instead of better. I'm trying so hard to love him…" Her voice trailed off, ending in a quavering gasp.

Kay burst out angrily, "Mama, you are afraid that the boys will do Dad in 'one day'! Just how much longer are you going to tolerate this? You never even report him to the police! There are other police stations. I know dad has friends at the local station. If he kills you there is no official record that you ever were abused. You are convinced that the good man we knew once upon a time is hiding in there; waiting to come back to us… it's not ginne happen, Mama! He's… going… to… kill… you! Open your eyes! The good ole days are gone! Gone! Long time! And they ain't… comin'… back."

Sylvia was sobbing and the girls were smarting!

"Why do you put up with it, Mama?" Olivia burst out. "We could leave him or have the authorities put him out!"

"You saw how he reacted to my request for a divorce…"

"Oh, Mama, asking for a divorce is like a challenge to his pride. You belong to him and he'll thrash his wife in his house with his fists or his whip when he feels like it. You think he's ginne be happy to hear, "Jordan, I want a divorce," hey, Mama?"

Kay and Olivia often spoke of how the love that once ruled over their family had turned to such bitter hatred! "You know something, Kay," Olivia once said to her, "I would be so excited if we got the news that Dad was picked up dead somewhere!"

Too late they realised their mother was at their door.

"Olivia! What a thing to say! He is your…"

"…Father after all, I know Mama, and you are my mother. Those marks and swellings on your face…when they go away perhaps the memories of how they got there will also disappear."

"Ma, why don't we just disappear…?"

"Where will we go, my baby? Just think of it. Six of you… and that makes seven with me…I can't go and leave you behind."

"You can go alone, Mama. He won't knock us around like he does you." Olivia spoke passionately. "We'll miss you like crazy but at least we'll know you're safe."

"Yes, Mama, please go away from here. We'll meet secretly when we can and you'll be fine. Oh, Mama, what if he kills you…how will we go on without you?"

"How would we live with a murderer father and a murdered mother?"

"I doubt it will go that far, my darlings," Sylvia actually looked faintly amused! "The Daddy deep inside still loves us and he…" Memories of the night he terrified her with his silenced gun caused her to trail off. She wondered what he'd done with the gun.

Kay gave an explosive, rude sound and stalked out, Olivia close on her heels.

"Can you believe Mama? "Who'll look after him?" she says. "He's your father," she says. "We can't throw him out," she says," Kay sneered angrily.

Now there she lay, in terrible pain and who knows what would happen next.

Abandoning the sleep battle, Kay and Olivia went to the kitchen. Over mugs of cocoa and Mama-made rusks, they reminisced.

"Remember the night he found a set of coloured dice that we overlooked…"

"Oooh, yes. We were so frantic trying to clear away the evidence of our game when we heard him arrive, no one noticed them…"

"He caught sight of the dice and accused Mama of teaching his children to gamble."

There was no sleep for anyone that night. They listened to the sounds almost the whole night through! They seethed with anger, sobbing in frustration. The boys dragged their mattresses into the girls' bedroom and they listened, crying and shivering and shaking, hatred and bitterness being reinforced. What they said in their anger, what they vowed in those horrible hours remained in their minds and hearts. Their anger was also directed at their extremely longsuffering mother.

James kept muttering, "One day is one day!"

"Just wait until I'm bigger…" Luke was so angry his voice was all choked up.

"Not until I'm finished," Zane said through gritted teeth.

"You guys, let's not talk about things like that. We have to pray for him." Sonja quavered tearfully.

"Sleep, poppet," Kay reached out and stroked Sonja's hair.

"I'm trying," she wailed, "but that noise…"

Then Kay's hackles went up!

"Enough is enough! When are we expected to sleep?" and with that she huffed out. Her siblings tried in vain to stop her. They listened in shocked silence.

Bang! Bang! Bang! She was as mad as a snake. The chair went right through the door panels. The splintering sound brought her siblings rushing out.

"Dad, do you think we're all deaf or dead? This noise is too bad. We want to sleep! It's almost time to get up for school already!"

"Go back to bed," Jordan growled. "Brave girl. She's now smashing my house down." He said calmly.

"You'll make a saint sin! Just please, keep quiet!"

And that brought the night's performance to an end. Once again, their mother lay there in horrific pain.

After a visit to the nearest hardware store the door was replaced. The manager, Mr Brown promised to forward the invoice to Jordan at his place of work.

Since no amount of make-up would improve her looks, Sylvia went out when the need arose and told whoever had the courage to comment, the same brief story, "My better half has a bad temper" in a tone that said, 'no more questions!'

The past just refused to stay buried!

Two nights after he'd walked out Jordan was back! He was in a shocking state. From the noisy exchange outside it appeared Taylor had accompanied him right to the back door. Jordan was very dirty with grass and mud all over his head, hands and clothes. His shoes were caked with thick mud. He stumbled right into his bedroom and keeled over onto the bed, full filthy kit. Sylvia cautiously slid off her side, quietly pulled a duvet from the linen cabinet in the corner and made a bed for herself on the floor between the bed and the wall.

"The kitchen door!" she sat up frantically. "I didn't hear it close. Can't trust that. I just hope Taylor isn't lurking around. He's also quite bonkers!"

Carefully she worked her way to the door and quietly opened it. The roaring from the bed overwhelmed any noise she made but she wasn't taking chances. The kitchen door stood wide open. She recognised the noise she was hearing – Taylor! He was swearing as he stumbled his way home in the dark out there. Slowly and nervously, she closed the creaking door, carefully twisting the handle so as to latch it silently when the door was in place. Then a rogue gust of wind snatched the door from her hand and slammed it shut. She jerked violently, fell back onto the door, and slowly slid to the floor with her hands over her face.

"My beating heart! Be still… H-h-h-hew! Almost jumped right out!" She didn't know whether to laugh or to scream.

Relief! No change from the bedroom din.

Back on her makeshift bed, Sylvia knelt at the window. She pulled the curtain over her and rested her chin on her arms on the window sill. She realised a storm was brewing. Thunder and lightning played wildly directly overhead. The peach trees just beyond the window wove wildly in the onslaught. Branches scraped eerily across the panes and roof tiles.

She hated this kind of weather. Then she was completely caught up in a reverie. Her father had been in the Second World War and he was terrified of lightning. He was shell-shocked her mother said and thunder and lightning were a reminder of the war and made him relive the horror. Her father had been where the fighting was at its worst in Africa. He was in Egypt during the siege of Tobruk. The bombing, the shelling and the noise of battle, sometimes lasting right through the night, stayed with him. The facts were vague in Sylvia's mind. Names she remembered were El Alamein; Tobruk; Alexandria and Egypt.

He played war games by himself using beans and mealies. The extremely rowdy game went on until he either got bored and went to bed, or he passed out right there at the table. His stash of beans and mealies were kept in a special spot and woe betide the entire household if they were not in their place when he looked for them. Those were the times she'd have to strap the youngest on her back, grab the others and run! Afterwards there were bruises to treat from being dragged to safety from a raging father who saw them as "the ruddy Germans". Sylvia conditioned herself to hide those cans and put them back when he entered the door. The toddlers were finding it hard to remember not to touch, and he kept them in an easily accessible spot.

During his lapses he entered another world, where his children were the enemy. Their mother was out of sight – asleep after the afternoon's bingeing. She would get hers when he finally turned in unless he was too drunk to even notice she was already asleep.

There'd be school the following day and before leaving the house a severe reprimand from her mother because she was the cause of the bruises the toddlers whined and moaned about. "Sylvie… she make me fall," was the snot and tears report. "Poor things," she thought, wiping her tears away, "They didn't know better."

Her dad had spoken a lot about life in the army and they soon learned to dread those talks because they would lead to an outbreak in the home…

"On those nights," she thought, "he'd 'a made us sit on his bedroom floor until the storm passed… still as mice. And that wasn't easy." Memories made her smile and wince softly. "Phew! Any sudden movement and the Major went into high hysterics."

Disturbing childhood memories… she shook them from her icy body.

Her Dad was a Sunday school picnic compared with Jordan…

He'd left following his last unspeakable acts of cruelty. A strange and uncanny air of relief mixed with fear had taken over. Who knew what was on the mad man's mind? Would he return with vengeance in his heart? Would he come back repentant? Unlikely! Would he stay away for good? Oh happiness…

And here he was – back again and as drunk as a skunk. As it turned out he never did fetch the suitcase James had left at the gate for him.

Relieved to see him leave, his upset family had huddled together.

"I wish he wraps himself around a lamp post… soon," Zane cried out fervently.

"Let's all go to bed," Sylvia had said tiredly.

"What if he comes back? I don't think I'll sleep a wink!" Kay had cried out.

"He may just break in quietly and come and kill us all. I don't think Dad is quite right upstairs," Luke had stated.

"Let's all sleep in one room and put up a booby trap over the door." Olivia yawned tiredly.

"Yes!" Sonja blurted out. "I know how that's made; I saw it on TV. What will we use...water or paint?"

"Water, lame brain!" Zane hissed at her.

"I know that," Sonja aimed a playful punch at him. "Of course, we'll use water."

"We? Oh no! James and Luke and I will be making it. You ladies go to bed... the girls' room... it's bigger. We'll come make our beds on the floor when we've finished." Zane did not often take charge but when he did, they listened and heeded.

School was out of the question the next day. Everyone was in a world of their own. It just all seemed so... so surreal. It was as if the previous night was a nasty nightmare if it wasn't for their mother's physical condition.

Now here he was, looking like a dog's breakfast...only worse.

Meanwhile Taylor got home from the fiftieth birthday celebration in mortal agony. He took the medication he still kept hidden in the console of his jalopy and went straight to bed. "No more," was his last thought.

Life at the de Vees went on as usual when Taylor was on the wagon. He came straight home from work each day and read the newspaper, sat around the house, watching television, finding it intensely annoying that his children treated him as if he was a nasty smell that had drifted in. No one spoke to him unless he addressed them by name. On one occasion he said, "Fetch me some tea, please." No one moved. They furtively looked at each other and then Cora asked, "Who's Daddy talking to?"

"To whoever wants to make me a cup of blasted tea!" he exploded. Elizabeth and Cora rushed out to the kitchen. "Is it only women and girls who make tea?" he sneered at the boys. "Huh? Can't boys make tea? What's those things hanging at the end of your arms? Huh? What are they? Vines? Pieces of wood? Huh? Boys who can't make a cup of tea…can they make anything else?"

Sidney boldly, though jokingly, said, "Making tea is girls' work, Da', not boys'."

"Bull!" roared Taylor. "Absolute bull! When I was your age, I did make my dad a cuppa tea every morning God give us, an' am I not a man? Huh? Tell me that. Am I not a man?"

He stomped to the kitchen archway. "How do you teach your churen? Is there boy's work and girl's work? If the girls can' chop wood, what if they marry a man who loses his legs? *Then* what they ginne do?"

"It may not happen…" I wish you lost yours long ago, she thought.

"Things happens, woman. What if these boys o' yours marries a woman an' she get sick, will they be able to make the poor girl a cuppa tea? Useless things…coming out' a my house!"

"Da' mustn't call us useless." Cohen called out behind him. "Maybe we take after Da'. I didn't yet see Da' get Ma a cuppa tea.

Maybe Da' made tea in his parent's home, but we never yet see Da' make Ma tea!" Cohen looked his father straight in the eye, defiance exuding from every pore.

"Cohen!" his mother was mortified. What if this outburst awakened the sleeping bear within the ratty, grouchy, bad-tempered, disagreeable sober man? The drunken brute they knew ... this nasty sober stranger?

"Leave him alone, woman," he roared. "See how you brought up my boys...they can't even show respec to they father!"

Sidney jumped up. "They...what did I say? It jus' so happens, Da', I agree with Cohen. I may as well admit it. Da' is like a bear with a sore backside! You terrify us! You are a terrorist!"

"Terrify? Terrorist? Your own father? This is your mother's doing, the dirty b..."

"No! Don't you call my mother dirty names. You are the dirty one. Have we ever seen you be nice to Ma? An' what about us? You treat us like we are unwanted adopted children."

"You talking rubbish... rubbish...proper rubbish! When did I treat your mother badly? When? Just tell me. Unwanted...adopted... Huh!"

His eyes were bulging, the ropes in his neck stood out alarmingly, but the boys were on a roll... they let their father have it!

"You are always drunk and full of fight. When you stop drinking, we see a new side and it is no better than the drunk, violent side." Anger rose. "How many times have we had to run around... from you... our fa-*ther*... chasing us around wanting to harm or kill us. Where do you think we go when we have to run for our lives? Huh? How many times have we got up at night when Ma is screaming for you to leave her alone? Where do you think she gets the black and blue marks she always has on her body? Huh, Da', don't tell me you don't remember. We hate you! I hate you! You are a rotten father!" Cohen ran out of steam.

"An' Da' pretends to be Jordan's friend but you threaten to burn down his house, family an' all, if we go sleep there. Where does Da' think we went to sleep when we had to run off in the night?" Sidney's voice was deadpan. He looked right into his father's eyes and the man had the grace to flinch.

Elizabeth stared at them in shock. What should she do? What should she say? Taylor looked like a cornered rat. Who would he spring at? She waited with bated breath.

Then, to the utter amazement of them all, Taylor threw back his head and laughed. He roared wildly, flinging his arms in the air, swinging them round and round as if to ease the wave after wave of crazy laughter that came from the depths of him. Cora came running in with the tea tray wobbling dangerously in her hands.

"Hoooooo," he screamed, "hooohoooohooo. Haahaahaa." At one stage it was the whistling scream of a train going through a tunnel. They just stared, stricken, like rodents in the hypnotising glare of a reptile. He writhed on the couch, holding his stomach, wiping the tears that ran freely down his cheeks, slapping his pate wildly. Up and down his feet pumped; then he fisted his knees rapidly until the paroxysm ended.

"Here… give me my tea, let me drink. My boys are men. They can talk to me man-to-man, now. In future I am Taylor! You hear me? Don't you Da' me ever again. Go on, say it!" he barked at Sidney and Cohen.

106

"Taylor," they both boldly stated.

"Good," he slurped his tea loudly. "Don't forget it." Turning to Cora, he said, "This tea is cold! You better let your mother teach you how to make decent tea!"

"That is very funny, Da' but I don't feel like laughing. When you used to drink you didn't allow us to make you tea, only Ma. And you shouted at her if the tea was hot. Suddenly today you want me to make you tea. I just don't understand you." Cora began to cry.

"Crying's not ginne do nothing. You can cry from now till next Wednesday, this tea'll be even colder. Here! Go make me a decent cuppa tea, an' don' tell me long stories."

Elizabeth stood and stretched out to take the cup from him.

"No!" he roared, "Not you! I want tea from my daughter!"

"Taylor, you are being absolutely insane!" Sidney shouted at him and Taylor looked at him and said, "Ah! My peer has spoken! Isn't it wonderful? It took me thirty-nine years to reach this age and it's taken you… how long? Sixteen years… fifteen? And it calls me insane."

He became almost docile, folding his arms, crossing his legs, one leg wagging slowly to and fro, head tilted to one side, gazing at his son. "Why don't we take this outside and settle the matter for once and for all." He may just as easily be asking Sidney to pass him the salt.

"Yes, why don't we?" Sidney's mouth hardened. His mother grabbed hold of his arms and pleaded with him to run to the Madden's and sleep there. He shook his mother's hands off saying that he was not afraid, and that if his father mauled him, it would go to show just what kind of a rotter he was.

"Even the Bible says parents must not provoke their children…" Sidney did not finish his sentence.

His father dived at him. "Spew out the Bible at me, will you? I'll show you!" and he grabbed his son by the scruff of his neck and yanked him outside. The family set up a frightened yell and Cohen raced to the kitchen. He returned with a rolling pin. He struck his father smartly across the head and the crazed man slowly sank to the ground.

Elizabeth helped Sidney to his feet. "He got me unexpectedly," Sidney said.

"And I got him unexpectedly," gloated the triumphant Cohen. "I hope the dog is dead!"

"Cohen! That's your father. Let me see how he is. Ooh…he's bleeding… he's bleeding."

They dragged him inside and Elizabeth bathed his wound, soaked it in iodine which had him awake and screaming. He soon settled down when he realised he was being doctored. She plastered it and he went to sleep. "I hope he isn't concussed," she told herself. "He has to be sober for this to happen!" The irony was bewildering.

For a while Taylor kept to himself. He did not ask who struck the blow to his head. He spoke to no one, not even to his wife. He made a bed for himself on the couch and remained a silent member of the family. The silence prevailed to the utter exasperation of his family who could not stand the tension. When Taylor got in from work it seemed a thick fog of hostility preceded him through the door. It left when he left for work the following morning. Elizabeth and the children were on tenterhooks, waiting for the day he would get home drunk yet again and the few inhibitions he had when sober, would dissolve again.

"The sound of silence is most disturbing," Elizabeth thought over and over. In other circumstances the silence would've been companionable.

Jordan lay on his back, eyes closed, the morning after the fiftieth birthday celebration and thought of the night before. He worried that he had been belligerent again. He was determined to build some kind of relationship before he sent Syl off to her happy hunting grounds. He smiled at the memory that thought brought on – he'd loved cowboy and Indian movies way back when. Happy hunting grounds.

He may have realised his mistake about his timing, but he said nothing about it.

Taylor had his policy, too. They would be a happy pair. Their happy hunting grounds were right here – on Planet Earth. He began to laugh then caught himself. Shh… he must remain quiet for now. Later he'd get up and go to work.

The days went by and Jordan worked the garden he'd started when he came from prison when he tried to pretend to be a reformed man. His mind was a cesspool of plans to begin his widower status.

He acted as nice as he was able. To return to what it was like at the beginning was out of the question. His mind was not what it used to be. Liquor had indeed taken its toll. That policy drove him. It was a fan that he waved across his fevered brow when he was frustrated, toiling in the garden after his day of toiling at work. It made him smile. The end was close – he felt it in his bones. Soon and very soon...

Meanwhile Taylor had been an' gorn an' dunnit again. He shook his head even as he laughed out loud at the man's foolishness. Had he no respect for his decomposing innards at all? Looked like his policy was a waste.

Taylor certainly had been and gone and done it again. They were seated around the table, playing a board game when Poppy smiled sweetly at her father and said, "I thought Da' stopped with the drink. Why do I smell drink an' it's coming from Da'?"

Taylor reached over and backhanded her.

Pandemonium broke out!

Elizabeth, who had reached the kitchen, raced back. Her sons were handling their father and losing the battle. The savage bear was unleashed!

Elizabeth hastily backtracked to the kitchen, grabbed the rolling pin and hurried back to deliver a damaging blow to her husband's head. She held the thing in both hands, raised it high and wham! It delivered a glancing blow to the side of his head for he moved just as she came in to land. Thinking this was curtains for her, she threw the rolling pin down and, screaming for help made a run for it. Cora grabbed the rolling pin, gave it to Sydney and he put it to better use.

When he lay there, unconscious, reality sunk home. What if he died? Big trouble. They must get help. "He's still breathing," Elizabeth said, holding a dampened hand close to his nose. "Get help... hospital... now!"

They got Jordan's help. Taylor was taken to hospital. He was badly concussed. Elizabeth explained to the hospital authorities that they had suffered a break-in!

When Taylor recovered consciousness, he looked around him vacantly, with a frown on his face. Then his eyes alighted upon Elizabeth and he sighed. "Ja-nee; I should'a known you'd be here. Hoping to see me take my last breath? Sorry to disappoint you. I'm still here, large as life."

"You are awake. I'm so glad." Elizabeth was genuinely relieved.

"Why? Why you glad? You wanna kill me right here in the hossie? I don't think so."

He stretched an arm only to jerk it back with a wince. It had a few intravenous attachments to it. "What d' you wanna do? I'll do it for you." said Elizabeth.

"Push that buzzer…I want a nurse…I want you outa here and I wanna make a statement to the police."

Quite agitated, Elizabeth jumped to her feet. "As you will; but push that buzzer yourself! I leave my distressed children alone at home to be with an ingrate like you," she spat at him. "What will you tell the police that your children won't be able to defend? Protecting themselves from attacks from their drunken father? Children sick of witnessing their mother being beaten up? Just what *will* you tell the police? I'm sure the police have had it up to here with drunken fathers assaulting their own families! You disgust me! Cursed was the day I said 'I do' to you. From now on I certainly do not! Get that nurse to find you alternative accommodation; you're not welcome to return to us." With that she flounced out, feeling strangely elated to have had the courage to tell him off. She felt free. She was smiling when she got into the taxi. Her companions in the taxi moved far from the woman laughing and crying hysterically.

That evening a solemn Jordan visited Elizabeth. He had visited Taylor after work. The man begged Jordan to ask Elizabeth's forgiveness on his behalf. He was begging her not to leave him. He was repentant and wanted to start a new life with her. He was deeply ashamed that he had pushed his children and possibly his wife to the verge of murder. He was also shocked to the core that she knew about his horsing around at the "Cow Shed."

That's what he wanted his wife to be told.

"He really means it, Elizabeth, I just know he does. By now I know Taylor, and I saw the look in his eyes." With hangdog demeanour Jordan pleaded his mate's case. "If he goes back on his word, I'll sort him out myself!"

"Sort what out? Are you in a position to help or advise him? Tell me that Jordan. With due respect, can you answer me truthfully? When we lie here dead why would you want to sort him out? I've had all the apologies I ever want to hear from that monster. If you believe a word he says, more fool you! If he told me that grass is green and the sky is blue, I would not believe him!"

"I can understand your anger. I know I was a monster. I would do anything to roll back time, but life just doesn't happen that way. Please give my friend another chance. They are letting him out of hospital later today and I promised to fetch him. Please, Elizabeth, please." He had his hands pressed together against his chest as though in prayer.

She pursed her lips and stared at him out of narrowed eyes. "I've got a bad feeling about this, Jordan Madden, a really, really bad feeling. Corpses are going to be taken out of here, you mark my words… remember my words." Her face became quite strange when she uttered those words. She looked at Jordan and with ill grace said, "Yes, fetch his Lordsh*t. Master of the Manor. Tell him his loyal servants…his lowly chattels await eagerly his return. We promise to be at his beck and call as always."

She then hung her head and looked at him feeling ashamed of her outburst. "Forgive me; you do not deserve my stupid sarcasm. I'm just so at the end of my tether!"

Two weeks later the well-behaved husbands and fathers decided to give their families a nice surprise.

The plan was to go into central Johannesburg, leave the children at a movie house with enough money to make them happy, and to take their wives on a trip to the circus which had arrived in town. It would be a lover's outing. The children would have excitedly joined them but they were promised tickets for the week-end.

The film the young ones would see was all the rage and they were as excited as all get out! They could hardly believe their fathers would be so good to them. It had never happened before. What sounded dodgy was that they would entertain their wives on their own. Each of their children had doubts but deliberately set them aside. "Benefit of the doubt…" was the general murmured decision.

"I wish I didn't smell a rat," Sylvia thought, trying hard to keep from frowning.

"This I gotta see," Elizabeth was thinking, her forehead deeply furrowed. She was praying that she'd be able to pretend to be on a lover's outing with a man she loathed.

They were dropped off at the highly decorated circus main gate with a polite-sounding word about their need to get pizzas for them which were less expensive than the circus restaurants.

"So, they need to go for pizzas in separate cars! What do I smell here?" Olive turned and watched the cars speeding off.

"The same unmentionable thought that's running through my corrupted mind. We'd better be on the look-out, maybe an assassin has been hired that your dearly beloved befriended in jail."

"True, hey. Let's go have a ride on that merry-go-round. Today we're children again." '

Taylor followed Jordan as they wended their way from the circus area.

As Sylvia said afterwards, "I felt then already, like we were off to a funeral – a very sad one – maybe our own funeral."

Elizabeth made a sound in her throat and said, "I wanted to say something but I couldn't think of a word to say. The silence was getting *so* loud! Taylor was humming a tuneless thing that sounded eerie… spooky. It gave me the deep heebie-jeebies. Brrr!" Her whole body shuddered.

"Ja, hey, I began to be suspicious especially when Jordan broke into a strange-sounding giggle every now and then. Sounded like a hyena in those wild life movies."

"Frightening."

"A hyena with its greedy little eyes on its prey."

"Exactly. But the tables turned nicely on him!"

"In a way they were hoist by their own petard."

"Shakespeare lives again. Long live Shakespeare."

"We've been talking about funerals. I wonder who invented that word with *fun* right at the start." Liz said.

"Must be the same one who put *fun* into funfair. Let's enjoy ourselves." Olive was quite serious. They'd made up their minds to enjoy their unexpected time there and both won prizes – a doll and a teddy bear.

They found out soon enough why they had to get a taxi back home from the circus.

They remained silent until they reached the cemetery gates. The double hearse in front of the mourners' coach seemed to beckon sickeningly.

"I wanna be sick," groaned Elizabeth.

"Liz! Pull yourself together! Here…" she handed over the bottled water that was in the holder in the door "… drink… a slow sip."

Liz took a deep breath and sipped a small sip.

The children were in two cars behind them.

"What a good thing we had these burial policies," Sylvia muttered softly. "Those lousy creatures are having a decent burial. I'd'a just buried the dog in tomato boxes banged together. And happily, I may add. After the years of suffering… Huh!"

"You make me want to laugh again. The dogs! No, that's an insult to dogs. Leaving us at the zoo like that and disappearing. Just what was behind leaving us there, I wonder. Supposedly off to get pizzas!... liars! Did they have a hit man on hire to do away with us? We'll never know, now, will we? Anyway... they got their rewards."

"Lizzie, my dear, if they had an inkling of what'd happen, they'd have made another plan and we'd be dead instead. What a thing, trying to beat the train across the track. Those boom gates have been broken for ever! Phew! What was Taylor thinking trying to overtake Jordan – right there... with the train hooting so loudly, too!!! That train driver is so traumatised, poor thing."

"Serve them right! Playing chicken with a train! Drink must've ruined their ability to see straight."

"They refused to show us what remains they were able to collect of our dear departed..."

"Excuse me... not-at-all-dear departed and never-to-be-missed.... Welcome widowhood... peace at last."

Sylvia sighed deeply. "I'm ginne pretend for all I'm worth at the reception afterwards, because that policy Jordan took out is ginne make me a greatly restored, *financially* that is, woman. The children are big now – I can leave them alone. I'm off on a luxury boat cruise at the end of the year."

"Ja nee. I was thinking along those lines, too. I just wish I could feel an ounce of gratitude to him. The wicked thing! Planning to kill me and benefit from it. I shall certainly enjoy spending all that moolla."

The cars were all finding parking place. The mourners' coach they were in came to a stop and the children joined them to walk to the grave sites together.

Mmap Fiction and Drama Series

If you have enjoyed Daddy, *Please Don't Kill My Mama,* consider these other fine books in **Mmap Fiction and Drama Series** from *Mwanaka Media and Publishing:*

The Water Cycle by Andrew Nyongesa
A Conversation..., A Contact by Tendai Rinos Mwanaka
A Dark Energy by Tendai Rinos Mwanaka
Keys in the River: New and Collected Stories by Tendai Rinos Mwanaka
How The Twins Grew Up/Makurire Akaita Mapatya by Milutin Djurickovic and Tendai Rinos Mwanaka
White Man Walking by John Eppel
The Big Noise and Other Noises by Christopher Kudyahakudadirwe
Tiny Human Protection Agency by Megan Landman
Ashes by Ken Weene and Umar O. Abdul
Notes From A Modern Chimurenga: Collected Struggle Stories by Tendai Rinos Mwanaka
Another Chance by Chinweike Ofodile
Pano Chalo/Frawn of the Great by Stephen Mpashi, translated by Austin Kaluba
Kumafulatsi by Wonder Guchu
The Policeman Also Dies and Other Plays by Solomon A. Awuzie
Fragmented Lives by Imali J Abala
In the Beyond by Talent Madhuku

Zororo Risina Zororo by Oscar Gwiriri
Sword of Vengeance by Olatubosun David
Finding A Way Home by Tendai Mwanaka
Your Epistle by Solomon A Awuzie
The Restless Run and Ruin of the Roaches and Rats by McLayode
The Reign of Terror by Ntando Gerald
Ibala Lyabwina Nama by Austin Kaluba

Soon to be released

Conversation with my Mother by Wonder Guchu

https://facebook.com/MwanakaMediaAndPublishing/